A NEW IRELAND:
A NEW UNION

A FIVE YEAR REVIEW

BY PAUL GOSLING

© Paul Gosling 2018, 2020, 2025
First published 2018
This edition, *A Five Year Review*, 2025

Published by
Colmcille Press, Ráth Mór Centre, Derry BT48 0LZ
Managing Editor Garbhán Downey
www.colmcillepress.com
Layout and design by Joe McAllister

ISBN 978 1 914009 49 5

Colmcille Press gratefully acknowledges the support of Creggan Enterprises Limited.

The moral rights of the authors and contributors have been asserted in accordance with the Copyright, Designs and Patents Act, 1998.

A CIP copy for this book is available from the National Library of Ireland and the British Library.

All rights reserved. No part of this publication may be reproduced or transmitted in any form or by any means, electronic or mechanical, including photocopy, recording, or any information storage or retrieval system, without permission in writing from the publisher. The book is sold subject to the condition that it shall not, by way of trade or otherwise, be lent, re-sold or otherwise circulated without the publisher's prior consent in any form of binding or cover other than that in which it is published and without a similar condition including this condition being imposed on the subsequent purchaser.

CONTENTS

Chapter One: Introduction — 5

Chapter Two: Dysfunctional Stormont — 19

Chapter Three: The Republic of Ireland — 31

Chapter Four: Health Services, North and South — 36

Chapter Five: Comparing the North and South — 40

Chapter Six: Reforming Public Services on an all-island basis — 52

Chapter Seven: The Subvention Conversation — 58

Chapter Eight: The Brexit Effect — 75

Chapter Nine: The All-Island Economy — 78

Chapter Ten: Foreign Policy — 83

Chapter Eleven: Social Attitudes — 86

Chapter Twelve: The Shared Island Initiative — 89

Chapter Thirteen: The Good Friday Agreement — 96

Chapter Fourteen: What might Irish unity achieve? — 110

Chapter Fifteen: What opinion polling tells us — 115

Conclusion: Preparing for a Border Poll — 118

Acknowledgements — 124

About the Author — 125

Sources — 126

CHAPTER ONE
INTRODUCTION

How far Ireland is on the journey towards unity is both unclear and strongly disputed. Indeed, many unionists would and do argue that it is not at all on that path. They suggest that the United Kingdom is both politically and economically stronger than the Republic of Ireland. Moreover, they believe that the gradual demographic change that reduces the proportional strength of Protestantism and unionism is not on the scale necessary to reorientate Northern Ireland away from its position within the United Kingdom.

However, republicans and nationalists strongly disagree. Moreover, unionism is in political retreat, no longer in control of Northern Ireland. Sinn Fein is the largest party within the Stormont parliament – an institution often referred to in previous times as a 'Protestant parliament for a Protestant people'. Former Northern Ireland prime minister James Craig spoke of "a Protestant Parliament and a Protestant State" and "a Protestant Government for a Protestant people" – contrasting this to the Catholic domination of the Irish state.[1] But it is clearly true both that the Irish state is no longer controlled or dominated by the Catholic church, nor do the Protestant denominations now dominate the North.

At its formation in 1921, Northern Ireland had a strong Protestant majority – 61.4% of the population was Protestant and 34.4% Catholic.[2] In the most recent census, 2021, Catholics had become 42.3% of the population, compared to 16.6% Presbyterian, 11.5% Church of Ireland, 2.3% Methodist and 6.9% other Christian, with 1.3% other religions and 10.1% no religion.[3] On that basis, Protestant denominations represented either 30.4% if the 'other Christian' faiths are excluded, or 37.3% if included. By either measure, Catholics now outnumber Protestants in Northern Ireland.

This changed demographic is reflected in electoral politics. In the 2022 Northern Ireland Assembly elections, Sinn Fein won 27 seats; the DUP won 25 seats; Alliance 17; Ulster Unionists 9; SDLP 8; TUV 1; People Before Profit 1; and independents 2. This provides unionism with 37 seats; republicanism/nationalism with 35; and non-aligned with 18. Votes were distributed across the parties, with Sinn Fein gaining 29.0% of first preferences; the DUP, 21.3%; Alliance, 13.5%; UUP, 11.2%; SDLP, 9.1%; TUV, 7.6%; Greens, 1.9%; Aontu, 1.5%; independents and others, 3.7%.[4]

Whether considered by number of votes or number of Assembly seats, unionist support was greater than that for republicanism and nationalism, but was less than 50%. Consequently, Northern Ireland can legitimately be described as a place of three minorities – unionists, republicans/nationalists and others. Those others constitute people of no religion, of non-Christian religions, but also people who prioritise turning their backs on sectarian outlooks and religious traditions.

The broader question of identity can be considered through the 2021 Census results, which demonstrate a stronger demographic trend against the tradition of British identity. Of the 1.9m residents, 606,263 (31.86%) describe themselves as 'British only'; 554,415 (29.13%), consider themselves as 'Irish only'; 376,444 (19.78%) call themselves 'Northern Irish only'; 151,327 (7.95%) regard themselves as 'British and Northern Irish'; 33,581 (1.76%) are 'Irish and Northern Irish'; 28,050 (1.47%) are 'British, Irish and Northern Irish'; and just 11,768 (0.62%) describe themselves as 'British and Irish'. In addition, 141,327 (7.43%) are 'others'. Northern Ireland is truly a shared place of various traditions.[5]

These demography statistics raise a core question: to what extent do the institutions of Northern Ireland reflect the reality of it being a shared place, which recognises those varying – and in the past conflicting – traditions?

The Good Friday Agreement of 1998[6] attempted to produce that shared place, recognising differing identities. However, Northern Ireland has significantly changed since 1998. At that time, it was overwhelmingly a country of two identities. Its solution to the conflict embedded recognition and rights based around those two identities. Today, Northern Ireland is a country with a wider range of identities. That section of the population that is neither unionist nor republican, and neither Protestant nor Catholic, is now much larger than it was in 1998. The GFA is situated in the Northern Ireland of 1998, not that of 2025.

As a result, there is a growing demand for the GFA to be revised and modernised, to reflect contemporary society. But even on the terms of 1998, it has arguably not been fully realised. Not least there is resistance within parts of unionism to fully accept that the GFA provides the basis for a referendum for Irish unity. Former UK minister for Northern Ireland Steve Baker has suggested – based on his Brexit experience – that the threshold for Irish unity should have been set at 60% of those voting.[7] Even the former deputy leader of the SDLP, Seamus Mallon, argued that the terms of the GFA for deciding the constitutional future of the North – a simple majority – should be amended to become a sort of 'super majority'. Former DUP MP Ian Paisley jnr went further and sought to legislate for a 'super majority' to change the constitutional status of Northern Ireland. However much they wish for those arrangements to be changed, they are firmly set within the GFA and it seems implausible that these will be amended.

1. (1) It is hereby declared that Northern Ireland in its entirety remains part of the United Kingdom and shall not cease to be so without the consent of a majority of the people of Northern Ireland voting in a poll held for the purposes of this section in accordance with Schedule 1.

  (2) But if the wish expressed by a majority in such a poll is that Northern Ireland should cease to be part of the United Kingdom and form part of a united Ireland, the Secretary of State shall lay before Parliament such proposals to give effect to that wish as may be agreed between Her Majesty's Government in the United Kingdom and the Government of Ireland.

Realistically, given that the GFA recognised the right of voters to opt for Irish unity, it also implied that preparations for this outcome should be made. If that was unclear, the chaos that followed the Brexit vote provides an obvious example of what happens if there is no preparation. 'Fail to prepare, then prepare to fail' is a business management mantra. However, David Cameron is reputed to have instructed his civil servants not to prepare for a 'yes' outcome to the Brexit referendum, on the grounds that he believed that it would make that outcome more likely. As a result, the British government had no blueprint for how to deal with the result. That uncertainty was added to by Cameron's immediate resignation after the outcome was known.

By contrast, the Irish government took the sensible decision to prepare for a Brexit leave result. Consequently, it was able to take a stronger position in negotiations, leading to what many regard as a more favourable outcome for the Irish state.

"Preparing is important," said Jonathan Powell on the prospects for a referendum on Irish unity. Powell was Tony Blair's key negotiator in the talks that led to the GFA. His comments were made in 2022 to a joint committee of the Oireachtas (Irish Parliament) on the Implementation of the Good Friday Agreement. "Refusing to talk about the issue is almost certainly a mistake." It is, he suggested, important to learn from Brexit, where the population didn't know what they would get.[8]

Powell has also, more contentiously, suggested that increasing numbers of unionists are becoming open minded about Irish unity because of the negative impacts of Brexit. In an interview with Civil Service World magazine, Powell said: "What you seem to have now in the North – and I wouldn't exaggerate it – is a feeling among many Unionists, middle-class Unionists in particular, who voted against Brexit, that actually when they come to look at this now maybe it's not such a great idea for their economic interests to stay out of the Republic of Ireland if the Republic of Ireland is going to be in the EU and the Single Market and they'd be out. You actually hear people in rugby clubs and golf clubs talking about this, which you never had before and if you think about the percentage that voted against Brexit, that wasn't a Catholic vote, that was a Protestant vote as well as a Catholic vote."[9]

Most controversially of all, in 2020 following Brexit, Powell suggested Irish unity was possible within a decade. "In Northern Ireland, once you put a border between Northern Ireland and the rest of the United Kingdom, Northern Ireland is going to be part of a united Ireland for economic purposes, that will increase the tendency for a united Ireland for political reasons too. I think that will happen within ten years . . . I think there is a good chance of a united Ireland within ten years."[10]

Review

36. After a specified period there will be a review of these arrangements, including the details of electoral arrangements and of the Assembly's procedures, with a view to agreeing any adjustments necessary in the interests of efficiency and fairness.

It is possible for the GFA to be reviewed and revised – as, indeed, happened through the St Andrew's Agreement.[11] And elements of the GFA have never been implemented – the Bill of Rights for Northern Ireland – while others are no longer implemented – the Civic Forum.

However, it is not plausible to believe that a consensus could be achieved around changing a simple majority for Irish unity, to a super majority that favoured unionism. Quite simply, a 'super majority' would de facto mean that a unionist vote counted for more than a republican/nationalist vote. It would breach the basic principle of the GFA of equality of esteem.

Yet it is clear that the GFA did not lead to stable, competent and efficient government. (See Chapter One.) Government has been suspended for 40% of the period since the GFA. It consists of representatives of two traditions that have been engaged in distrust over centuries, with some of their members involved in armed conflict. While the same could be argued regarding the Irish state in terms of its traditions and history, it has achieved a stable and efficient government in recent years.

One of the most contentious areas of the GFA was over the creation of cross-border bodies. In practice, this outcome has been one of the most disappointing. It has been suggested that David Trimble was particularly exercised by these and he almost refused to the sign the GFA over their creation.[12] Several areas of activity that were to have been established under the governance of cross-border bodies were ultimately removed in order to achieve cross-party agreement. (One of these was reportedly a cross-border body overseeing higher education, while the Irish government blocked a move for a cross-border body promoting inward investment.[13])

It is surprising that there is no obvious political pressure for an expansion in the number of cross-border bodies. These might in themselves assist with a prospective process towards Irish unity. However, it might equally assist in improving competence and efficiency in both jurisdictional areas, and need not in themselves create assumptions of constitutional change. The DUP has been particularly touchy with regards to increased cross-border co-operation. It has, for example, resisted calls for co-operation between Invest NI and IDA Ireland[14] and been reluctant to support a connection between the Wild Atlantic Way and the Causeway Coast[15]. By contrast, Ulster Unionist Party representatives have taken a more pragmatic approach to cross-border co-operation in recent times.[16]

Amendment or reform of the GFA would seem necessary if one current political demand is upheld – for the UK to withdraw from the European Convention on Human Rights. This has been proposed by former Conservative Party leadership contender Robert Jenrick and also by Reform UK. Their objective is to circumvent decisions by the European Court of Human Rights in relation to the treatment of some migrants arriving in the UK. However, the ECHR is integral to the GFA, potentially creating a conflict between the GFA and proposals to reform legislation removing the UK from the ECHR. This situation is made more serious by the GFA being agreed under international law, with both the UK and the RoI governments being signatories.

Nor should the wider context of English politics be ignored. A significant proportion of membership of both the Conservative Party and Reform UK have limited commitment to retaining Northern Ireland within the United Kingdom. This reflects the dominance of England and English nationalism within parts of UK politics; the perceived closeness of Northern Ireland to European politics, especially given its special status within the Single Market; but also because of the subvention for Northern Ireland, which is regarded as a drain on the English economy and tax base.

(Brexit was predicated on saving the cost of the UK's contribution to the EU budget, instead spending that domestically. The net contribution to the EU was £9bn annually, or £13bn prior to receiving EU spending in the UK.[17] The current official subvention from Westminster to Northern Ireland exceeds those figures.)

A 2019 opinion poll found that 20% of Conservative Party members would be 'very' or 'fairly' happy for Northern Ireland to leave the UK. But this rose to 59% of members, if this had been the alternative to Brexit not happening.[18] (Even more, 63%, prioritised Brexit over retaining Scotland within the UK.) This suggests that the modern Conservative Party is very focused on England and English interests, with the concept of a 'one nation' party a thing of the past. There has, over the past two decades, been a more general and strong increase in the number of people in Great Britain who emphasise their English or British identities, despite the parallel growth in the non-white and foreign born population.[19] [20]

Reform UK's attitude to Northern Ireland and Irish unity is ambivalent. In the last General Election, Reform UK entered into an electoral alliance with hard line unionists, Traditional Unionist Voice. But Reform UK leader Nigel Farage personally endorsed two DUP candidates (Ian Paisley jnr and Sammy Wilson) against TUV candidates. Farage himself has both indicated that he expects Irish unity to happen 'one day'[21] and also distanced himself from that same prediction[22]. However, his party's support for leaving the ECHR could increase support for Northern Ireland leaving the UK. Reform UK is growing in popularity in Britain and it is plausible that it could either lead or be a member of UK government within the next few years.

Within the environment of Irish politics, there are conflicting indications of direction of travel. Fianna Fail's Shared Island initiative has made important contributions to both cross-border relationships and support for Northern Ireland and cross-border projects. But Sinn Fein has again underperformed in a general election against its own expectations of reaching government. As even some supporters of Sinn Fein recognise, it is essential that other parties – not just Sinn Fein – advocate for Irish unity in the near term. Over-dependence on the fortunes of one party is not good for the cause of unity. Ironically, it is in the interests of Sinn Fein's ambitions for Irish unity that the SDLP survives while advocating for unity, a former Sinn Fein election candidate Chris Donnelly has suggested.

Former Taoiseach Leo Varadkar has made particularly strong statements of support for the principle of Irish unity, suggesting progress towards its planning as an objective, not just a long term aspiration.[23] In an interview with RTE he explained: "I believe we are on the path to unification. I believe that there will be a united Ireland in my lifetime."[24] Varadkar also put forward a proposal previously made in our book 'A New Ireland' of a two stage referendum process, with an initial vote relating to the principle and a second on the post-negotiation detail. This arrangement has been rejected by leading academic Professor Brendan O'Leary as unfeasible and not practical under the terms of the GFA.

'A New Ireland' was first edition published in 2018 with a second edition in 2020. It made a significant impact, but given the events subsequent to its publication, there is a need for a refresh of the situation. Our book suggested a Ten Point plan to prepare for Irish unity, some points of which have now been addressed. Those ten points were:

1. **Seek agreement on the size of the UK government's subvention for the cost of Northern Ireland as part of the United Kingdom.** Subsequently, the cost of the subvention has increased as a result of the Covid pandemic – which reduced tax revenues – and for other reasons. A number of academic studies have considered the size of the subvention, notably those from Professor John Doyle of Dublin City University and separately from Professor John FitzGerald of Trinity College Dublin and Professor Edgar Morgenroth of Dublin City University. We report these conflicting arguments in a later chapter.

2. **Address Northern Ireland's infrastructure deficit by increasing capital spending on public sector infrastructure.** While there has been some progress on major public projects since 2018, it is difficult to argue that there has been a strategic focus on infrastructure improvement or, indeed, sufficient overall improvement in key infrastructure. Positive improvements have

included the completion of a new dual carriageway A6 road for large sections between Belfast and Derry and agreement on a new A5 road between Strabane (and possibly Derry) and Aughnacloy, the cost to be shared between the Northern Ireland Executive and the Irish government. There have also been improvements to the electricity grid and new privately financed wind and solar farms. In addition, Ulster University's new Belfast campus has been opened, investment promised to expand its Derry campus (some funded by the Irish government) and significant investment in new further education campuses across the North. A new bus and rail depot in Belfast has represented a major allocation from Northern Ireland's capital budget, while the new York Street rail station has opened. Despite these successes, the infrastructure gaps remain more obvious than the new investments. Those gaps include substantial weaknesses in the North's water supply and sewage outflow systems, which are blocking new commercial investments and house building, as well as causing serious environmental damage, especially in Lough Neagh. This is one factor, but not the only one, in the failure to meet demand for new homes, especially in the social housing sector, with exceedingly long housing waiting lists. Public transport remains a weakness, with Belfast a very congested city. The York Street interchange remains a significant blockage in the road system in the North. Despite these challenges, the main public sector crisis in Northern Ireland is in its health service. The main difficulties are with demand for services that cannot be met within its system. However, the cost of outdated infrastructure and its inflexibility eats into the health budget, both denuding the available funding of services, while also increasing the cost of service provision. The shortage of centralised services leads to poorer patient outcome and wasteful expenditure on outdated building stock. The Bengoa review concluded that too much of the health budget goes into maintaining buildings, including those that are not fit for purpose. Without dedicated funding to reform the NHS in Northern Ireland, including to replace outdated buildings and create a modern digital infrastructure, then the cost of delivering an NHS in the North will likely be too great to bear.

3. **A reduction in public sector workers to the proportionate level of Great Britain and the Republic of Ireland.** While there have been redundancy programmes within the Northern Ireland Civil Service, it is noticeable that much of the public sector has been unable to recruit and retain skilled staff as required. This applies to some key senior and professional staff in the Northern Ireland Civil Service and most especially to the health service. Ulster University's Economic Policy Centre observed that in the first quarter of 2024 there had been employment growth, which had largely been met through incoming migrant labour.[25] This suggests that Northern Ireland is failing to create the skilled workforce required for the modern labour market; that too many high skilled workers and potentially high skilled students are leaving Northern Ireland to study and work elsewhere; and that Northern Ireland is suffering as a result of a disproportionately large number of people who are economically inactive (in part because of the problems within the NHS, with many people unable to work because they are on long health waiting lists for treatment). Reliance on inward migrant labour to fill job vacancies has exacerbated social tensions in some areas, expressed through increased conflict for housing and racist street disturbances. Northern Ireland has a significantly larger public sector as a proportion of total population, compared to all other UK nations and to the Republic of Ireland. (See table below.) This is despite Northern Ireland having the longest health waiting lists and the biggest problems in various parts of the public sector (such as water, which is not part of the public sector in England or Wales.) While part of the explanation is that Northern Ireland is the smallest of the UK nations, and therefore suffers diseconomies of scale, it also suggests that it suffers from a lack of public sector reform. Merging the public

sectors of the two Irish jurisdictions would achieve efficiencies of both outcome and scale.

4. **Improved direct links between education and industry, leading to a more competitive market-oriented economy and increased employment rate.** There are mixed results in this regard. Linkage with the private sector by the universities and also the further education sector appears to be strong. However, the connections between schools and employers can be weak – and school-based careers guidance is too focused on higher education, including in British universities, rather than pupil-focused best advice. This should involve greater recognition in the value of vocational skills, of which many employers in Northern Ireland are very short. Northern Ireland is at nearly full capacity in terms of its labour market. Official claimant count unemployment at December 2024 was 3.5%, which is regarded as effectively close to full employment. It was less than the UK-wide statistic of 4.2%. However, these statistics are misleading and it is more informative to consider the employment rate statistics. As at February 2025, the employment rate in Northern Ireland was 72.1%, whereas that in the UK as a whole was 74.9%.[26] This reflects in part the higher number of people in Northern Ireland who are unavailable for work, for reasons of ill health, disability, caring responsibilities and full time education. Those who are unavailable for work are disproportionately short of the higher level skills and vocational skills most valued by employers. In October 2018, Northern Ireland's employment rate was lower at 69.5%. While recent statistics show an important improvement, there has been UK-wide employment growth. There remain serious shortages in the skills most desired by employers in Northern Ireland.

5. **IDA Ireland should promote investment and business performance for the whole of the island of Ireland.** While this has not been achieved, there are signs of improved relationships between IDA Ireland and Invest NI including the first ever

joint trade mission.[27] Both agencies report having practical difficulties in working together in border areas because of differences in data recording, for example in reporting on skills in cross-border travel to work areas.[28] More needs to be done in promoting the all-island economy, recognising the mutual benefits of a strong economy on both sides of the border.

6. **Reform of Northern Ireland's education and health systems and reform of the Republic's health system.** In recent years there has been significant, but slow, progress in the South in extending free provision of healthcare to a larger proportion of the population, in line with the agreed SláinteCare plan. Meanwhile, Northern Ireland's healthcare system has worsened year by year. Waiting lists and waiting times have extended and even the private sector is struggling to cope with healthcare demand. Little progress has been made in implementing the Bengoa reforms, without which the crisis gets ever worse. Nor are there obvious signs of increased co-operation between the two jurisdictions to achieve economies of scale and greater centralisation of specialist services to improve patient outcomes. Northern Ireland's education system remains based on academic selection, which delivers often excellent results for those pupils who attend grammar schools, but poorer outcomes for pupils in the non-selective sector. The Republic achieves better educational outcomes in terms of the proportion of the population with a graduate degree and vocational skills, and also improved school pupil retention.

7. **A harmonised corporation tax rate.** Under international pressure, the Republic has increased its corporation tax rate for global businesses to 15%, rising from 12.5% in 2021. The main rate of corporation tax in the UK (including Northern Ireland) rose in 2023 from 19% to 25%. The gap between the South and the North has therefore increased from 6.5% to 10%. In response, a number of Northern Ireland firms have now located bases – or moved head offices – to the South.[29]

8. **A single and integrated Ireland would have a more successful economy and achieve economies of scale.** There are signs as a result of Brexit that the all-island economy has grown, driving some economies of scale and reshaped all-island logistical arrangements.

9. **Political agreement on a new all-island jurisdiction within the European Union.** As a result of Brexit, Northern Ireland has a different, closer, trading relationship with the EU than has Great Britain. Northern Ireland remains part of the Single Market for goods, which has created a partial trade barrier with Great Britain in relation to some items. Northern Ireland is therefore subject to some regulations that are determined by the European Union, despite Northern Ireland not having direct political representation within the EU.

10. **The European Union to be asked to assist with the reunification of Ireland within the EU.** Despite allegations to the contrary by some unionists, this has not happened. Nor could the EU politically intervene in this way, unless this had the support of the British and Irish governments following, presumably, border polls that indicated that the populations of both the North and the South supported reunification.

In summary, there has been progress towards closer relationships between North and South, but less progress than advocates of reunification would want. Brexit had the result of requiring changes to trading relationships between Britain and Northern Ireland, as there was no practical means of protecting the EU's Single Market while keeping an open border within the island of Ireland, unless some trade restrictions were introduced between Britain and Northern Ireland. This has led to increased all-island trade, some limits to Great Britain to Northern Ireland trade and improved economic relationships within the island, on a cross-border basis.

The period of Boris Johnson's premiership was notable for political tensions between the British and Irish governments, as well as between the UK and EU. Under Rishi Sunak and Keir Starmer, relationships have improved: between Starmer and both Micheál Martin and Simon Harris they seem to be warm and affable. Relationships between the Irish government and parts of unionism remain difficult. However, Ireland's Shared Island Unit has helped to improve some cross-border infrastructure and service provision.

POPULATIONS OF UK NATIONS:	
UK	68,265,200
Northern Ireland	1,920,400
Scotland	5,490,100
Wales	3,164,400
England	57,690,300
[Source: ONS[30]]	
NUMBER OF PUBLIC SECTOR WORKERS PER NATION:	
UK	5,851,000
Northern Ireland	227,000
Scotland	596,000
Wales	329,000
England	4,927,000
[Source: ONS[31]]	
PROPORTION OF PUBLIC SECTOR WORKERS TO TOTAL POPULATION:	
UK	8.57%
Northern Ireland	11.82%
Scotland	10.86%
Wales	10.40%
England	8.54%

Number of public sector workers (whole time equivalents) in RoI: 388,448[32]
Population of RoI: 5,149,139[33]
Proportion of public sector workers to total RoI population: 7.54%

(Note: Any reduction in public sector employment in Northern Ireland to bring it down to comparable levels in Ireland and England can be expected to take place over a number of years, facilitated through retirements. Unification with Ireland is likely to be a gradual process.)

CHAPTER TWO
DYSFUNCTIONAL STORMONT

Northern Ireland has the highest proportion of public sector workers for its population of any of the nations of the UK and Ireland. It also has by far the longest health waiting lists and waiting times (a later chapter will examine in detail the health services crisis). Waiting lists for social housing are absurdly long. Water services are so poor that construction of new homes and commercial facilities has been on hold in much of the North, while it is a major factor in the unlawful pollution of Lough Neagh.

But rather than talk in headlines, let us look at public services, one by one.

HOUSING

There is a dire shortage of housing in Northern Ireland, including in social housing. The number of households on the social housing waiting list has almost doubled in two decades, while the number of social homes allocated has drastically fallen. In 2002/3, there were 26,248 outstanding applications for social housing, by 2023/4 this had risen to 47,312. Meanwhile the number of allocations fell in the same period from 12,150 to 8,156.[34] At this rate it would take six years to clear the applications – except new applications are being received constantly, with an increasing proportion of these being households in stress.

The Northern Ireland Housing Executive is constrained from building the necessary new social housing because of its status as a public body. If it were reconstituted as an independent not for profit agency it would be able to use its revenues and assets as leverage for loans, enabling it to build new public housing. Institutional stasis at Stormont has delayed agreement on changing its legal status, though ministers are seeking approval from the UK government to enable NIHE to borrow against assets and revenues.

WATER

The construction of new social housing and of commercial redevelopment is seriously constrained because of the inability of NI Water to build new water supply and waste water facilities. In addition, the poor quality of existing waste water infrastructure is leading to high levels of sewage discharge into the sea, rivers and worst of all, Lough Neagh, contributing to what is an environmental disaster in the largest lake in the UK or Ireland.

According to the Construction Employers Federation, Northern Ireland needs to spend in excess of £640m a year to catch-up with water underinvestment in NI. In the 2022/23 year, less than half this – £309.5m – was invested in new assets and the network. NI Water recognises that it needs to spend at least £500m per year for the next decade "to meet the current and rising environmental standards and facilitate economic development".[35]

NI Water's chief executive, Sara Venning, wrote in its most recent annual report: "We have draft public expenditure limits from Government for 2023/24 which are below the levels required and have no visibility of funding for the final three years (2024/25 to 2026/27) of PC21 [price controls set by the Utility Regulator]. Such a position would not be tolerated in any other part of the UK." At the time of the annual report's publication, the Assembly was down and ministers were not in place – but the underfunding crisis remains despite restitution.

One solution is 'mutualisation' – transferring ownership from government to customers. This is the model used successfully in Wales, Glas Cymru. The same type of structure is used in Northern Ireland for the Moyle electricity interconnector with Scotland, which is operated by Mutual Energy, as is the gas transmission pipeline from GB to NI. This structure would enable NI Water to borrow on the markets, with loans secured on revenues and assets. Glas Cymru is able to borrow at advantageous rates because of these securities. However, this solution has been blocked in Northern Ireland because of opposition by Sinn Fein and the DUP.

EDUCATION

Northern Ireland is often claimed to have one of the best education systems in the world. But that is a simplistic and misleading description. Schooling is based on academic selection at age 11, which often rewards pupils from higher income families at the expense of children from deprived backgrounds. That divergence tends to continue through a person's adult life and career. Another problem with the North's education system is reflected in weaknesses in higher level vocational skills and a shortage of undergraduate places compared to the number of school leavers entering higher education. While 56% of the RoI population 25 to 64 have a degree[36], just 30.7% of adults in that age range in Northern Ireland have a degree.[37]

Despite this, a report from the Nuffield Foundation concludes that pupils in Northern Ireland on average outperform those from the other UK nations. "Pupils in Northern Ireland lead the way among UK nations in most measures of pupil outcomes, even moving ahead of the region of London, which is often widely revered for its high level of educational attainment. The highly positive outcomes displayed by pupils in Northern Ireland through the EPI study are more positive than seen in other international comparisons."[38]

While Nuffield's assessments suggest that Northern Ireland's school system is in some regards more effective than that of Britain, it underperforms compared to the Republic of Ireland. A report[39] from ESRI concluded: "There are marked differences in educational attainment between Ireland and Northern Ireland," most notably that the North suffers from having a higher proportion of school pupils with low levels of educational attainment. ESRI adds: "Ireland and Northern Ireland perform well in international comparisons of skill development at primary and secondary levels. The two jurisdictions have broadly comparable patterns of skill development and similar patterns are evident by social background, indicating comparable levels of inequality in skill development."

The big problem in the North is the de facto drop-out of pupils in teenage years, especially those who attend non-selective post-primary schools. Enrolment rates in education for 15 to 19 year olds in Northern Ireland in 2022 was 71%, compared to 92% in the Republic. "Early school leaving is two to three times higher in Northern Ireland compared to Ireland and this gap has widened over time. The proportion of 16-24-year-olds who leave school with at most a lower secondary qualification is 14% in NI compared to 6% in Ireland. This is concerning as early school leavers are more likely to be non-employed or work in low wage and potentially insecure jobs later in life. Furthermore, students from more disadvantaged backgrounds are more likely to be early school leavers in Northern Ireland than in Ireland. This highlights an important difference between the two systems, and it is likely that academic selection in Northern Ireland and the success of the Delivering Equality of Opportunity in Schools (DEIS) programme in Ireland in retaining students in education are strong contributory factors."

ESRI suggests that higher pay levels in the South create a greater incentive to educate to graduate level. Its report added: "Students from disadvantaged backgrounds are more likely to be clustered in certain schools in NI compared with Ireland. Being channelled into non-grammar schools leads to low educational expectations relative to those who attend a grammar school, particularly for boys from socio-economically disadvantaged backgrounds. This lack of aspirations, particularly amongst disadvantaged boys, was reiterated as an issue by stakeholders in NI."

ESRI's analysis points to problems in Northern Ireland in delivering equality across the education system, which is unsurprising given its use of academic testing that favours pupils from higher income families. But even without abolishing academic selection, a greater focus of support for children from deprived backgrounds prior to first attending school is likely to achieve improved outcomes. Withdrawal from the education system at a young age is a particular challenge for the Northern Ireland system and tends to contribute to higher rates of economic inactivity and lower productivity for the society as a whole. There also needs to be a priority placed on increasing the provision of vocational skills training at a range of ages.

TRANSPORT

Transport policy in Northern Ireland has been heavily criticised over many years, in particular with regard to poor provision of roads, rail and, in some instances, buses in the North West and South West. At its worst, the A5 road has had a tragically high number of fatal road accidents. Repeated delays have, in part, been blamed on administrative failures by the Department for Infrastructure, and its predecessor the Department of Regional Development, including failure to undertake all legal obligations related to environmental assessments of the planned road.

Public transport is another weakness, with fares sometimes higher in Northern Ireland than in the Republic.

The absence of a more effective public transport system, combined with Belfast containing a disproportionately large number of jobs and student places, has caused the city to be the 50th most congested in the world. Belfast has 18.3% of Northern Ireland's population[40], yet 30% of the jobs[41]. It is the fifth most congested city in the UK, despite being only the 14th [42] or 22nd [43] largest (depending on method of calculation).

ENVIRONMENT

Northern Ireland is a disaster zone when it comes to environmental protection. The worst example – one of the worst in the whole of Europe – is the degradation of Lough Neagh, which is covered for much of the year by green algae bloom, which blights its natural habitat and led to warnings not to walk dogs on its shore.[44] Causes include the pumping of raw sewage into the lough by NI Water, run-off from agricultural fertilisers – supported by Stormont's Going for Growth policy – and industrial activities.

Another instance of woeful policy making was Northern Ireland's Renewable Heat Incentive (RHI). This provided subsidies for the burning of wood, in order to reduce the use of oil and gas for commercial heating. However, the subsidies were set at a level higher than the cost of the wood – thereby promoting wasteful wood burning ('cash for ash'). It was also counter-productive in terms of energy use, as well as being a significant cost to Northern Ireland without achieving its objectives of promoting environmentally friendly energy sources. Many businesses that signed up to the scheme ended up substantially out of pocket after the rules were changed retrospectively.

A globally significant failure of environmental protection is the Mobuoy illegal waste dump[45], on the outskirts of Derry. The site is leaching poisonous chemicals into underground water reservoirs and possibly to the neighbouring River Faughan, representing a threat to the city's drinking water supplies. Failure to effectively regulate and control the site led to around a million tonnes of waste being illegally dumped and an estimated £100m of landfill tax revenues being evaded.[46] Further hundreds of millions of pounds – the latest estimate being £700m[47] – will have to be spent to make the site safe. Its current dangerous state prevents the construction of the section of the upgraded A6, connecting the section from Drumahoe to the Foyle Bridge. The waste area is one of the worst illegal dumping sites in Europe – and may in fact be the very largest.

POLICING

Reform of policing is sometimes referred to as the greatest political success of the Good Friday Agreement, yet the PSNI remains unaccepted to parts of the nationalist/republican community and often struggles to function amidst the demands on it. Despite the continuing internal employment imbalance towards Protestants and unionists, the PSNI is alienated also from parts of loyalist working class society and it remains unable to gain control over loyalist paramilitary groups.

PSNI chief constable Jon Boucher claims that his service is underfunded by £37m a year at present, leading to staff shortages and an inability to provide the level of policing service that keeps the public safe. He said: "We have got to make sure we get the numbers back to what they should be because we have, in effect, broken the workforce. The PSNI is a jewel and we have got to make sure we do not allow it to go into further decay. We need to ensure we survive this year and get recruits in."[48]

In 2023, PSNI officer numbers were the lowest in its history, at 6,730 full time officers and 214 part time reserves.[49] Boucher says his service should have around 8,000 officers and at least 7,000. He described officers at being at 'breaking point' from over work.[50]

The Patten review of policing[51] was intended to create a new era for Northern Ireland, putting behind the negative attitudes to the former RUC. However, critics argue that too much of the old RUC culture continues to pervade the PSNI. This came to the fore most contentiously with criticisms of former chief constable, and former RUC officer, George Hamilton.[52]

Despite the PSNI being established in 2001, large numbers of its current officers and staff were previously employed by the RUC. This, critics say, contributes to associations with the old RUC and fails to create a reformed culture.

A series of Freedom of Information requests revealed concerning information about the current composition of PSNI officers and staff and the limited impact of policing reforms.

Question: How many police officers currently employed by PSNI were previously employed as officers by the RUC?

Answer: As of 23rd September 2024 there are 524 police officers and 111 part time reserve officers with date of appointment prior to 4th November 2001 [the date of formation of the PSNI]

Question: How many civilian staff currently employed by PSNI were previously employed by the RUC?

Answer: As of 23rd September 2024 there are 880 civilian staff with date of appointment prior to 4th November 2001.

Question: What is the religious background of PSNI officers?

Answer: As of 1st December 2024:
Perceived Protestant	65.97%
Perceived Roman Catholic	32.62%
Not determined	1.41%

Question: What is the religious background of PSNI civilian staff?

Answer: As of 1st December 2024:
Perceived Protestant	78.75%
Perceived Roman Catholic	18.90%
Not determined	2.35%

Question: What is the percentage of ethnic minority PSNI officers and civilian staff?

Answer: As of 1st December 2024:
Police officers	0.69%
Police civilian staff	0.71%

Question: How many PSNI officers are members of notifiable organisations, broken down by organisation?

Answer: 350 PSNI officers have declared membership of a notifiable organisation:
Ancient Order of Hibernians	1
Apprentice Boys of Derry	23
Freemasons	132
Independent Orange Order	6
Knights of St Columbanus	1
Loyal Orange Institution	94
Royal Black Preceptory	42
Others (not specified)	51

Question: How many PSNI civilian staff are members of notifiable organisations, broken down by organisation?

Answer: The PSNI does not hold this information.

These statistics confirm that the PSNI still has a long way to go to generate confidence across society that it is a balanced organisation.

JUSTICE

The justice system in Northern Ireland is in serious crisis, leading to prosecutions being delayed and abandoned. A recent review by the Northern Ireland Audit Office concluded: "A key feature of how the system in Northern Ireland has operated has been a failure to complete cases within reasonable timescales. Crown Court cases in Northern Ireland typically take more than 500 days from the date an offence is reported until a verdict is delivered in court, twice as long as in England and Wales. Around 12% of Crown Court cases in Northern Ireland take in excess of 1,000 days to complete."

The NIAO continued: "Since 2006 there have been several independent reports (particularly by the Criminal Justice Inspection Northern Ireland) which have been critical of overall performance and identified a number of issues. The key causes of delay are weaknesses in the early stages of investigations. The progress of cases through the system is punctuated by practices and processes that are not efficient and work against timely delivery of justice. This has a significant impact upon the quality of service to citizens and impacts upon the confidence of the public in the system's effectiveness.

"The inability of justice organisations to commit fully to a collaborative model of delivery underlies this situation. These organisations have not been able to overcome the undeniably difficult challenges which prevent true collaboration. The justice system has lacked key components of the infrastructure necessary to support collaborative working, in particular, a common performance framework.

"In addition to the impact upon victims, defendants and witnesses, there is a significant financial cost of avoidable delay. However, justice organisations are not currently able to quantify the financial cost of delay. Attempts to improve performance are not supported by detailed financial analysis to quantify the expected costs and benefits . . . . The key performance issues affecting justice have been known for at least a decade and are not insurmountable."

The damning conclusion of the NIAO was "Currently the criminal justice system in Northern Ireland does not deliver value for money. The cost of criminal justice in Northern Ireland is significantly higher than in England and Wales, with no additional benefit arising. Cases take considerably longer to complete than in England and Wales.

"These performance issues have arisen in an administrative environment which has lacked key components of the infrastructure which criminal justice organisations need to operate collaboratively as a whole system. Until these are introduced, it is unlikely that the criminal justice system will deliver improved performance and value for money.

"It is widely accepted that the criminal justice system cannot function effectively until the various justice organisations work more closely together. This will require behavioural change, supported by effective collaboration within the Criminal Justice Board (CJB) and the Criminal Justice Programme Delivery Group (CJPDG). This includes establishing clear lines of accountability; quality information systems; and a transparent reporting framework. The system needs to demonstrate substantial improvement in the matter of avoidable delay, which should be subject to continuous review."[53]

In short, the justice system operates in much the same way as the rest of the Northern Ireland public sector – above average costs, below average performance, poor value for money and weak collaboration between key partners.

SUMMARY

At its heart, the dysfunction in public service delivery in Northern Ireland is the result of the dysfunction of the Executive, with ministers from different parties finding if often impossible to work together. As one commentator put it, 'mandatory coalition in Northern Ireland puts ministers together with opposing world views – it's like having the British government operating under a coalition led jointly by Jeremy Corbyn and Nigel Farage'.

There have been times when government in Northern Ireland has been built on apparent mutual respect. Relationships at present between First Minister Michelle O'Neill and deputy First Minister Emma Little-Pengelly are good, as were those between Ian Paisley snr and Martin McGuinness. But too often, the Executive has appeared to be, as one former secretary of state reportedly put it, 'civil war by other means'.

At times, government ministers have barely been able to speak to each other because of mutual animosity, in particular between DUP and Sinn Fein representatives. But relationships between departments at the level of officials can also be fraught, with institutional difficulties in working across silos. Some public services – social care, childcare and environmental protection, for example – connect policies, budgets and responsibilities of various departments. Without effective departmental partnerships, delivery is hampered.

The worst instances are hopefully in the past, but previous decisions can have long and expensive tails. Peter Robinson's so-called 'letter from America'[54] caused institutional crisis and continuing wasteful costs. In 2013, while away in the United States, the then first minister Peter Robinson wrote to end progress on the redevelopment of the old Maze/Long Kesh prison site. This was to have hosted a multi-sports venue, significant commercial ventures, but also a visitor centre using parts of the former prison. Robinson decided that the risks of this becoming a 'republican shrine' were too great and redevelopment was largely put on hold.

Twelve years later, the Maze remains mostly undeveloped. It is a 347 acres site that was expected to create a major economic boon for the Lisburn area. The development of a multi-sports venue would have saved money that was instead pumped into soccer and rugby stadiums, while leaving the GAA Casement Park a source of political acrimony. Ultimately, no one has gained from the impasse, with serious fiscal, economic and social negative outcomes.

Without shared visions, mutual respect and a commitment to make decisions beyond the traditional sectarian boundaries, it will be impossible for Northern Ireland to be a modern and efficient state – whether Stormont be located as a decision-making body within the UK or a united Ireland. Stormont remains focused on tribal division, not on reconciliation, service delivery and efficiency. Those outlooks are endemic and would not change simply by transferring the existing, dysfunctional, parliament into a different jurisdiction. Suggesting the retention of Stormont within a united Irish state is absurd.

CHAPTER THREE
THE REPUBLIC OF IRELAND

For many international observers, the Republic of Ireland's reputation has not recovered from the banking collapse in 2008/9. Today, however, Ireland is regarded as an above average, well managed, state. By many measures it outperforms the United Kingdom, which has struggled to implement Brexit and cope with the consequences of it.

The OECD provides a comparator of its member states.[55] Ireland has a higher level of trust in its government amongst its population than most OECD members and more than that registered for the United Kingdom. (50.6% of Ireland's population have a high or moderately high level of trust in its government, compared to 34.8% in the UK and 41% across all OECD members.) The UK performs best amongst OECD members for 'green budgeting' for climate change: Ireland is second. Both countries perform poorly for the advancement of women in society, with the UK outperforming Ireland.

Ireland performs particularly well, the OECD reported, in terms of its people's satisfaction with its education system, at 84%, compared to 72% in the UK and 67% across OECD countries. Ireland spends below the OECD average on public procurement, at 7.7% of GDP in 2021 compared to 12.9% on average across the OECD and 15.7% in the UK.

However, the World Bank reports that Ireland has the highest levels of (private sector) investment per capita of any country in the Europe and Central Asia region, at $31,436.[56]

In the IMD International World Competitiveness rankings[57] Ireland is ranked fourth, behind Singapore, Switzerland and Denmark. The United Kingdom is 28th.

While Ireland has the world's third highest GDP per capita[58], it is generally recognised that in the case of Ireland GDP is not a useful measure of economic performance because of US multinationals that locate their tax base in Ireland. Using the more accurate GNI* measure, Ireland is 15th.[59]

The collapse of Ireland's financial system in the 2008 crash revealed its weak regulatory system, as well as its dependence on and integration in the global financial system. Without a bail-out and EU membership, Irish society would have collapsed. And the process of recovery was harsh and painful, causing much resentment against the banks and the global financial system. Even as part of the recovery, Ireland was picked to pieces by vulture funds.

Ireland has now recovered from the 2008 financial crash. Much of the state's funding of the Irish banking bail-out has now been recovered. At the time of writing, Ireland and the UK have comparable government credit ratings. However, Ireland is poised for an improvement and the UK for a possible downgrade.

Membership of the European Union protected Ireland from the 2008 crash developing into a total collapse of its financial system. Its continued membership of the EU – unlike the UK – is seen as one of the strengths of the Irish state and potentially influential in any future referendum on Irish unity. Equally significant, the Irish government conducted comprehensive preparations for a possible Brexit leave vote. In contrast, the British government instructed its officials not to prepare for Brexit in case this made a leave vote more likely. Consequently, Ireland was better prepared than the UK for Brexit and was arguably more effective in the subsequent negotiations because of this.

Ireland has settled into an apparently permanent situation of coalition government, containing a variety of political parties. The coalition of Fianna Fail, Fine Gael and the Greens in the period to 2024 delivered consistent and socially progressive policies, including on the environment. However, this led to a wipe out of the Greens and their replacement by more right wing independent TDs who seem likely to push back against socially liberal policies and practices. The new coalition between Fianna Fail, Fine Gael and independents, with a negotiated outcome facilitated by disgraced former minister Michael Lowry, has humiliated the government and seriously undermined its reputation. It is too early to predict the longer term ramifications for the Irish government's credibility.

Irrespective of the political make-up of the Irish government, the state's development into a socially liberal and economically successful society seems set. While there have been ground level disturbances from groups protesting against immigration this has not led to significant levels of support for overtly racist and far right political parties and candidates.

Substantial progress has been made in recent years by the Irish government in developing education and skills, welfare support and public infrastructure and in promoting economic development and inward investment. While pay is high, it is insufficient for large numbers of people in Ireland to afford a home. Both pay and the cost of living are at the top end of the European Union. Housing is a major factor in the costs.

The biggest failure of Irish government policy has been not matching the supply of housing to growing demand. This is a crisis for many young adults, even those in well paid jobs, who are unable to afford to rent or buy their own homes. Critics believe that this, at least in part, is a consequence of excessive reliance on market forces and private sector delivery. Increased provision of social housing, using the UK model, might have helped to redress this. However, a shortage of construction skills has also been a factor – which might reflect insufficient government intervention in the development of appropriate vocational skills.

Economic progress has been the result of deliberate policy and is linked to EU membership. Whether Ireland outperforms the UK in future years may depend to a large extent on how the EU meets current and future economic and foreign policy challenges and whether Ireland within the EU or the UK outside the EU is better positioned to deal with what seems likely to be a period of extreme turbulence as the United States becomes more insular. Ireland's substantial reliance on overseas investment and multinationals provides substantial employment and corporate tax revenues, but creates a serious vulnerability when international trade hits trouble.

It has been assumed that Irish unity would lead to improvements in the Northern Irish economy – a lower tax rate might quickly attract some footloose enterprises, for example. But other core elements of the Republic's economic success would take longer to produce benefits, in particular the successes of its education and skills policies, which could take a generation or two to produce a substantial benefit. There is also the risk that a section of the unionist population in Northern Ireland might leave upon Irish unity. It is difficult to speculate on the impact on the skills environment without detailed analysis of those parts of unionism most unwilling to accept a unity vote.

The Republic's population grew from 4.60 million in April 2014[60] to 5.38 million in April 2024[61] – an increase of 780,000, or 16.96%. Northern Ireland's population was 1.90 million according to the 2021 census[62], up from 1.81 million in the 2011 census[63] – representing an increase of around 90,000 people in the decade, or 5.0%[64].

While immigration and an enlarged population may create additional demand on housing and other infrastructure, it increases economic demand and can provide skills where there are job vacancies. The economic impact of migration is highly disputed and varies according to the skills profile of any immigrant population. A 2008 House of Lords report stated: "Our overall conclusion is that the economic benefits to the resident population of net immigration are small, especially in the long run."[65]

It has been estimated that the loss of highly skilled European workers following Brexit has had a significant negative impact on the UK economy, especially on productivity. In evidence submitted to Parliament, Professor Jonathan Portes explained: "the reductions in migration resulting from Brexit are likely to have a significant adverse impact on UK productivity and GDP per capita".[66]

A paper published by the Centre for Economic Policy Research explained: "For the UK, the estimated impact [of immigration] is that a 1 percentage point in the migrant share of the working age population leads to a 0.4-0.5% increase in productivity. This is higher than in most other advanced economies and reflects the relatively high skill levels of migrants to the UK."[67]

The additional demand created by a larger population itself creates an economic impact, which can be negative on housing but positive on the hospitality sector, for example. Inward migration also creates additional tax revenues for government, while also adding to demand on public services. It is reasonable to add that desire by people to move to a country is a vote of confidence in that destination country, but a vote that is not always welcomed by the existing population.

CHAPTER FOUR
HEALTH SERVICES, NORTH AND SOUTH

Northern Ireland's health service is in a crisis unmatched anywhere else in Britain or Ireland. Waiting lists in Northern Ireland are multiple times higher than those elsewhere, when weighted for population. (See Table One below.)

Media reports are full of stories of patients waiting in ambulances for hours outside hospitals, needing urgently to be admitted after road accidents, heart attacks and strokes. Those attending A&E typically have to wait many hours, sometimes for more than a day, before they can be treated or admitted.

The crisis is similar in general practice, where it is notoriously difficulty to gain an appointment. This is the result of a serious lack of GP coverage. The number of general practices in Northern Ireland fell from 350 in 2014 to 317 in 2023. During the calendar year 2023, 17 GP practices in Northern Ireland surrendered their contracts.[68] In the last eight years some 9% of GP practices in Northern Ireland have closed, with 16% of GP practices in the Western area closing.[69] According to the BMA, too few doctors are being trained to replace those GPs who are retiring.[70]

Patients unable to access treatment such as surgery can become unavailable for work. This is reflected in Northern Ireland's labour market statistics, which show that a higher percentage of the population are economically inactive than in the rest of the UK. Health incapacity is one of the main factors in this. (Northern Ireland's economic inactivity rate as published in January 2024 was 25.8%, of whom 39.3% were 'long term sick', comprising 10.2% of the working age population.[71] By comparison, the UK economic inactivity rate published in January 2024 was 20.8%[72], of whom 29.7% were long term sick.[73])

The problems within Northern Ireland's health service are leading to more people paying privately for healthcare, either through insurance, or else meeting the cost of private treatment upon diagnosis. The use of the private sector to deliver healthcare in Northern Ireland rose at a rate of 33% in one year[74], with a 55% increase in self-pay admissions between 2019 and 2022[75]. There are anecdotal reports that private healthcare demand has grown at such a rate that providers will often only serve patients covered by healthcare insurance, not those who are paying for themselves.

Yet a set of solutions is on the table. The Bengoa report[76] was published in 2016 and proposed substantial reforms to the NHS system in Northern Ireland. Too much of the NHS in the North is located in old and unsuitable buildings, too much of it in Belfast, too little is devolved and it has too few staff and inadequate investment in specialist services. Commissioning of services should be based more on value, with greater focus on primary, community and social care. Political stasis in Stormont has prevented the reforms being implemented as required.

Meanwhile, the Republic's gradual implementation of its SláinteCare programme is, using a phased approach, increasing the number of residents who neither pay to see their GP, nor for hospital treatment as an in-patient or out-patient. A review in the Oireachtas in 2017 of the Irish health system[77] recognised the need for change, moving closer to the UK's NHS via the SláinteCare 10 year programme (which is now behind schedule).

Ireland has a mixed private and public healthcare system. Private insurance is taken out by four out of ten people in the state. A third of people are entitled to medical cards, enabling them to have free prescriptions. A prescription charge is otherwise levied of €1.50 per item up to a maximum of €15 (€10 for people over 70) per month for each person or family.[78]

A visit to a GP typically costs €45 to €65. More than half the population of Ireland are now entitled to free access to a GP, including all adults over 70 and children under eight. A visit to accident and emergency is free if the result of a referral by a GP, but otherwise costs €100, while charges for in-patient stays in hospital were abolished in 2023.[79] There are 86 hospitals in Ireland, of which 67 are publicly administered.[80]

Healthcare cost and quality are likely to be a major concern in any referendum on Irish unity. While the personal cost of paying for healthcare is likely to be a barrier to a 'yes' vote in a border poll, waiting lists and waiting times in the Republic are much shorter than those in the North. Astonishingly, although the South has an insurance-based health provision system and the North has a system based on state provision of health services, government expenditure on health per capita is actually higher in the South than in the North. (The figures are €5,853 RoI, €4,739 NI.[81])

If the Irish government is genuinely committed to a united Ireland, it needs to progress the SláinteCare programme – which it should anyway, for the benefits of its existing population. But it also needs to consider the benefits of an all-island healthcare system. Both the North and South jurisdictions are of insufficient size to benefit from the possible economies of scale that could be achieved through merging the two systems. There are already examples of cross-border co-operation, including cancer care for the wider North West region operating from Altnagelvin hospital in Derry and heart surgery in Dublin for child patients from both jurisdictions.

Given the stronger financial position enjoyed by the Republic compared to the North, increasing cross-border health provision financed by the South would assist with service improvements for both nations, but could also generate significant goodwill in the North that would assist with future relationships and preparation for a referendum.

Table 1. - International Comparison of Waiting Lists, June 2023

	Inpatient		Outpatient		Inpatient + Outpatient	
	Inpatient/Day Case	Inpatient/Day Case >12 months	Outpatient	Outpatient >12 months	Inpatient + Outpatient (combined figures where available)	Inpatient + Outpatient (combined figures where available) >12 months
Ireland	109,186	15,375	597,101	139,881	706,287	155,256
Northern Ireland	119,095	62,856	416,022	203,682	535,117	266,538
Scotland	149,255	101,223	518,491	282,636	667,746	383,859
Wales	142,334	52,019	421,547	49,928	563,881	101,947
England	7,965,223	383,083	-	-	7,965,223	383,083
Per capita (million) population						
Ireland	21,408	3,015	117,074	27,427	138,482	30,442
Northern Ireland	62,577	33,027	218,594	107,022	281,171	140,049
Scotland	27,237	18,472	94,617	51,577	121,854	70,049
Wales	45,803	16,740	135,655	16,067	181,458	32,807
England	141,003	6,781	-	-	141,003	6,781

Note on sources: Table presents data from multiple independent country sources. Some figures are derived from official reports. Conceptual definitions of 'Inpatient' and 'Outpatient' may vary across countries. See the 'Data Sources and Methodology' section below for details

Source: FactCheckNI, reproduced with permission[82]

CHAPTER FIVE
COMPARING THE NORTH AND SOUTH

The Economic and Social Research Institute, based in Dublin, is an internationally respected body. In recent years it has conducted a series of reviews that have compared the economies, public services and outcomes of the North and South of the island. In doing this it has been assisted by finance from the Republic's Shared Island Unit and also from IBEC. ESRI's conclusions have been highly significant, making clear the improvements needed in both jurisdictions.

THE ECONOMY
Productivity

Productivity per worker in 2020 was approximately 40% higher in Ireland compared to Northern Ireland. In the period 2001 to 2020, the two jurisdictions diverged significantly, with productivity growing in the Republic, while it fell in Northern Ireland.

Productivity advantages favouring the Republic can be found in administrative and support services; finance and insurance; the legal and accounting sectors; and scientific research and development. Northern Ireland outperforms the Republic with regard to electricity and gas supply and construction.

Productivity variance can be explained by investment levels and labour market skills, including the proportion of workers educated to further and higher education levels. ESRI's model suggests a 1% increase in the share of graduates employed generates a 1% increase in sectoral productivity. The report found export intensity is another important factor in driving Irish productivity.

"Without a comprehensive strategy aimed at improving competitiveness among Northern Ireland firms, the reform of education and skills provision and increasing investment in isolation are not guaranteed to enhance Northern Ireland's productivity."[83]

Brexit

UK to EU goods trade was 16% lower, and trade from the EU to UK 20% lower, than it would have been as a result of Brexit. Global exports of goods from the UK grew slowly, probably partially a result of Brexit spillover effects on supply chains.[84]

Goods trade between Ireland and Northern Ireland grew substantially following Brexit. Of international flows (which do not include GB), some 35% of NI imports (€2.6bn) came from Ireland and 53% of exports go to Ireland (€5.6bn) in 2021. Ireland's imports in the same period were €99.8bn and its exports €160.3bn. Germany is the NI's second largest export destination, generating 15% of exports. Northern Ireland makes up almost 5% of Ireland's total goods imports and just over 2% of exports. The food and beverages sector accounts for a considerably larger share of cross-border trade than it does in the overall trade structure, with 24% of goods going from Ireland to Northern Ireland in this sector, and 27% of goods going from Northern Ireland to Ireland.[85]

Trade between Ireland and Northern Ireland rose considerably after January 2021, but fell between Ireland and Great Britain. Northern Ireland's share of total Irish imports increased from 1.5% in 2015 to 5% following Brexit. Northern Ireland's share of UK to Ireland imports increased from 6% to over 40%. Food and beverages has been the key sector driving the change. The share of Great Britain in total Irish imports declined from 23% in 2015 to 7.2% in early 2021. The share of Irish exports destined for Great Britain declined from 10.9% to 6.3%.[86]

There is concern about the impact of Brexit on SMEs involved in the manufacturing sector, some of which are dealing with changes to supply and logistics arrangements, as well as falls in demand from some traditional buyer locations. This impact is particularly felt in Mid Ulster.

Assimilation involved in the building of an all-island economy is leading to more companies in the North being bought by firms in the South: recent examples include Firmus, while Belfast City Council is promoting the city to investors in the Republic.[87] The Northern economy tends to be dominated by international businesses and smaller locally owned enterprises, with ambitious Northern companies expanding through selling their equity to external investors.[88]

Future economic modelling

ESRI is partnering with the UK's National Institute of Economic and Social Research (NIESR), supported by Ibec, to produce and publish a new macroeconomic model for Northern Ireland and the all-island economy. The initial report considered the development of a model for the Northern Ireland economy and how it can be used to produce economic forecasts and to examine the potential impacts of economic policies and shocks. Among scenarios to be considered will be the potential for more devolution in Northern Ireland, such as an income tax rate hike to increase investment and spending.[89]

The modelling framework can be also used to generate a baseline projection over the medium term. GDP growth in Northern Ireland is expected to average around 1.2% per annum over the medium term, similar to its longer-term historical trend, although it is projected to be somewhat higher in the short term. The challenge of relatively low productivity in Northern Ireland must be addressed through sustained productivity-enhancing investment to improve long term economic prospects and living standards. With growth in Ireland expected to moderate in the coming years from previous extraordinarily high rates, projections are for growth in the all-island economy to average around 2.2% per annum over the medium-term.

"Northern Ireland occupies a unique position following Brexit and the Windsor Framework. It is part of the UK fiscal, welfare and monetary unions – where the main policy levers are mostly exercised at a UK national level – along with its national economic policies for devolved administrations and regions. Simultaneously, it remains within the EU Single Market for goods with Dual EU/UK regulatory regimes, participates in the Common Travel Area (CTA) between the United Kingdom and Ireland and is supported by a commitment to continue specified areas of North-South cooperation. The economic effects of this will continue to evolve over time. Whatever the background situation, it is clear that the economies of both Northern Ireland and Ireland can have a mutually beneficial impact on each other through improved economic outcomes on both sides of the border and enhanced interaction."[90]

Housing supply

A study of housing supply in Ireland, Northern Ireland, Wales, Scotland and England found that in all markets, but especially Ireland, the traditional financial sector is not able to provide the requisite amount of credit for the necessary level of housing activity. Consequently, increased Government investment in the form of expanding the level of social and affordable housing stock available is a key factor across all markets. Labour shortages in the construction sector are a key challenge for the expansion of housing supply across all housing markets discussed, in particular in the UK. Reforms are required in planning processes, regulation of land speculation and the use of modern methods of construction, backed by training and education schemes, in the Irish and Northern Irish markets.[91]

Electricity market

Alignment of renewable energy targets in Ireland and Northern Ireland can lead to lower costs across the island. Ireland and Northern Ireland now have the same 80% renewable electricity target by 2030. There is a slight decrease in the profitability of renewable generation, but this arises as a result of lower prices across the market, and a net gain for consumers. Aligned targets also lead to higher deployment of renewable energy generation in Northern Ireland and higher investment in storage in Ireland. When the North-South interconnector is in place, it will facilitate greater energy transmission between the two jurisdictions, reducing the requirement to invest in storage. The interconnector would reduce the number of network upgrades needed.[92]

SOCIAL POLICY
Child poverty

Over the period 2004 to 2023, child income poverty declined in Ireland while rates fluctuated more in Northern Ireland. Throughout the period, income poverty rates were higher in Northern Ireland at 21% in 2021-2023 compared to 14% in Ireland. The two jurisdictions were closer in terms of child material deprivation, which was affected by economic boom and recession. Families on low incomes in Ireland have been less able to convert household income into an adequate standard of living compared with families at the same position in the income distribution in Northern Ireland. This could be attributable to a higher cost of living in Ireland. Children in lone-parent households, larger families, and households with a disabled member face significantly higher risks of poverty in both jurisdictions.

Household joblessness is a bigger risk factor for child poverty in Ireland than in Northern Ireland. In Northern Ireland, children in jobless households have a 10 percentage points higher risk of being income poor compared to those in households with at least one employed adult. In Ireland, children in jobless households are 27 percentage points more likely to be income poor than children in working households. Low education levels of the household head, significantly increase the risk of child poverty and material deprivation in both jurisdictions. However, there are more children in Northern Ireland living in such households.

While the welfare systems in Ireland and Northern Ireland are broadly similar, Ireland offers higher child benefit levels, whereas Northern Ireland provides broader access to means-tested benefits. Stakeholders in Northern Ireland identified the two-child limit in UK welfare policy as a major driver of child poverty. Mitigation measures designed to offset the Benefit Cap in Northern Ireland were identified as being crucial to preventing further poverty. In Ireland, the reliance on temporary cost-of-living measures was seen as less effective than sustained increases in social welfare payments linked to inflation.

Northern Ireland's provision of free school meals to children in low-income households is an important direct support, but there are calls to expand these benefits during holiday periods and make them universal. Stakeholders in Ireland welcomed the recent expansion of similar supports. Policies supporting access to education, training, and childcare are critical in both jurisdictions to improve parental access to employment and to address risks of low-wage work, particularly for lone parents and disabled individuals.[93]

Income Inequality

Income inequality, as measured by the Gini coefficient, is very similar in Ireland and Northern Ireland. Ireland's younger and more highly educated population leads to lower income inequality with relatively fewer people with no earnings. However, the higher and more unequal wages paid to workers in Ireland results in relatively higher market income inequality. Differences in the tax-benefit system influence the distribution of disposable income in Ireland and Northern Ireland. The Irish tax system is more progressive and reduces income inequality more than the Northern Irish tax system. But the level and coverage of means-tested benefits in Ireland is lower than Northern Ireland. Therefore, the Irish means-tested benefit system reduces inequality less than the Northern Irish means-tested benefit system. The combination of these two opposing effects results in similar overall levels of redistribution by the Irish and Northern Irish tax-benefit systems taken as a whole.[94]

Gender Disparity

Employment rates for women and men are lower in Northern Ireland, compared to the Republic. Labour force participation for women is 72% in the North and 76% in the South. Much of the difference is explained by educational attainment levels. Having children reduces women's employment level to an equal extent in the two jurisdictions. But women in the North with older children are less likely than those in the South to be in work. Being a lone parent reduces labour market participation in both jurisdictions, but it is a stronger barrier in the North. Older age is also a stronger barrier to participation for women in Northern Ireland. Women in both territories were likely to be low paid. Higher education protects women against low pay in both jurisdictions.

Women were significantly more likely to work part-time than men in both jurisdictions, but rates are significantly higher for women in Northern Ireland. Despite greater emphasis on job activation in the UK welfare system, lone mothers in Northern Ireland are less likely to be in the labour market. This points to issues beyond welfare disincentives, such as the availability of childcare. Tackling low pay among lone parents is vital to ensure that they are not activated into in-work-poverty.[95]

A report from Northern Ireland's Department for Communities points out that the gender pay gap in Northern Ireland is the lowest in the UK, which is related to the North's higher level of public sector employment.[96]

Migration

Ireland and Northern Ireland have experienced increased inward migration. A larger share of the working-age population in Ireland was born abroad (20%) than in Northern Ireland (9%), with the majority of migrants in both jurisdictions born in Europe. A minority of those born outside of the island are citizens of their new places of residence (Ireland or Northern Ireland). This share is greater in Ireland, where 35% of migrants are Irish citizens, than in Northern Ireland, where 17% of those born outside the UK are British citizens. In both jurisdictions, most migrant groups are highly skilled and more likely to have third-level qualifications than the native-born population, though the skills profile of migrants is generally higher in Ireland than in Northern Ireland. Migrants in both jurisdictions have high employment rates, particularly EU migrants. A higher proportion of migrants in both jurisdictions work in professional/managerial jobs than non-migrants. East Europeans in both jurisdictions are much less likely to be in professional managerial jobs.

In Ireland, there was little difference in either academic achievement scores or well-being at age 15 between migrant-origin children and their Irish-origin peers. In Northern Ireland, first generation migrant-origin children have considerably lower achievement scores in English reading and mathematics than their Northern Irish/UK origin peers. Second generation migrant-origin children in Northern Ireland have similar achievement scores but have lower well-being than young people of Northern Irish/UK origin. In 2017/2018, attitudes to migrants are more favourable in Ireland than in Northern Ireland. Brexit has increased difficulties for migrants engaging in cross-border travel, with a lack of clarity around rights and fear of immigration checks.[97]

EDUCATION AND SKILLS
Pre-school
Children in both jurisdictions are entitled to free universal pre-school provision, which have very high levels of take-up. Entitlement is to term-time, part-time hours in both systems, but hours are longer in Ireland (15 hours) than Northern Ireland (12.5 hours).

In Ireland mothers of young children work longer hours and are more reliant on formal childcare; in Northern Ireland mothers are more likely to work part-time and are more reliant on friends and family for care. In both jurisdictions, centre-based care is more common when mothers are employed and family income levels are higher.

Social inequalities in cognitive and socio-emotional outcomes are equally prevalent among young children in Northern Ireland and Ireland. In both jurisdictions, social background and home learning environment play a greater role in child outcomes than participation in ECEC.

Both systems face similar policy challenges around affordability for parents and the employment conditions of early years staff. Ireland and the UK regularly feature among the countries with the highest costs for full-time care in the OECD. There is significant scope for policy learning across the island of Ireland. Stakeholders highlighted the merits of the Sure Start system in Northern Ireland for its wraparound and integrated services for children living in disadvantaged areas.

The success of the Northern Ireland system in bringing childminders into the formal system offers a model for Ireland, where only a tiny number of this group are registered. The AIM programme that supports access to ECEC for young children with special educational needs in Ireland was commended by stakeholders from both sides of the border.[98]

Schools

School pupils' numeracy and literary skill levels are similar in the two jurisdictions, but qualification attainment is significantly better in Ireland. Early school leaving is two to three times higher in Northern Ireland, and this gap has widened over time. Both systems face challenges in tackling educational disadvantage. Stakeholders across the island spoke of the benefits of the DEIS programme in Ireland and those in Northern Ireland suggested a similar programme could reduce educational inequality in the North.

Students from disadvantaged backgrounds in both Northern Ireland and Ireland achieve lower grades than their peers from more affluent backgrounds. While this is more pronounced in Ireland in the Leaving Certificate cohort, this can be explained by more pupils in Northern Ireland leaving school at an earlier age.

Academic selection in Northern Ireland has a big impact on educational and career outcomes, especially for boys from poorer backgrounds. Students from disadvantaged backgrounds are more likely to be clustered in certain schools in the North compared to the South. Low levels of aspiration, particularly amongst disadvantaged Protestant boys, are a serious challenge in Northern Ireland. Northern Ireland has a smaller proportion of students in vocational, further education, courses. Ten per cent of the population in Northern Ireland have a further level qualification compared to 30% in Ireland.

At all levels of qualification, wages are significantly higher in

Ireland than in Northern Ireland. Higher pay related to education and qualifications can be an incentive to study and may help to explain higher qualification levels in the Republic and lower productivity levels in Northern Ireland. Stakeholders in both jurisdictions felt that further education is perceived as 'second-best' relative to higher education, which is potentially detrimental to students.[99] [100]

HEALTH

A key distinction between the healthcare systems of Ireland and Northern Ireland is the absence of a universal healthcare system in Ireland. In Northern Ireland, all residents are entitled to a wide range of health and social care services that are almost entirely free at the point of use, while in Ireland much of the population pay out of pocket for a range of healthcare services, including general practitioner (GP) and other primary care services. Relative to Northern Ireland, a significantly higher proportion of the population in Ireland are covered by private health insurance. Both systems currently face similar challenges, including increasing demand for healthcare services, increasing expenditure and workforce shortages.

There are higher levels of unmet healthcare needs due to affordability issues in Ireland relative to Northern Ireland. The most common reason for unmet healthcare needs in Ireland and Northern Ireland is long waits to access care. Both jurisdictions post-Covid have experienced a significant increase in the proportion waiting more than 12 months for out-patient and day and in-patient services, but especially in Northern Ireland. The proportion of those on the waiting list for more than one year has increased from 12% to 20% in Ireland and from 20% to 60% in Northern Ireland.

"The significant challenges currently being experienced in both systems – particularly in the areas of waiting lists and recruitment – might provide fresh impetus for at least exploring the potential for greater cooperation in relation to health matters. If greater cooperation on health policy and planning is to occur between Ireland and Northern Ireland, there is a need for significant reform in data collection and sharing."[101]

In addition to the ESRI reports, the Irish government has itself reported on comparisons between Ireland and Northern Ireland, noting that "Public spending on a per person basis is higher in Ireland in health, education and housing whereas Northern Ireland has significantly higher expenditure per person on social welfare."[102]

Pay for health professionals is significantly higher in Ireland than in Northern Ireland, playing a part in the difficulties faced in the North in recruiting and retaining qualified staff, including doctors.[103] The lack of spare capacity in the North's labour market has particularly affected the health service, which is consequently highly dependent on attracting migrant labour.[104]

OTHER ANALYSIS

In addition to ESRI, there have been other analyses that compare circumstances in Ireland and Northern Ireland. The paper 'Social Security in a Unified Ireland' by Professor Mike Tomlinson[105] provides explanations on the different benefits, taxation and pensions systems in the two jurisdictions.

Tomlinson writes: "Across the island, a million people receive a state pension and 1.5 million children are supported through child benefits, and this scale of provision is clearly evident in public accounts. In Budget 2021, social welfare payments in Ireland accounted for more than a quarter of public spending; in comparison, such spending takes up about 40 per cent of Northern Ireland public expenditure. It is the scale of the latter that contributes to the myth that Britain's subvention to the north is so great as to make unity unaffordable. It is argued here that not only are current commitments to social security provision in the north manageable financially, but there is also scope for enhanced provision in the transition to a unified system."

Paul Gosling, in a paper for ARINS, 'Who is Better Off?'[106], used information from Tomlinson and other sources to explain that state pension and welfare support systems provide more support, on balance, in the South than in the North. "The UK is an outlier for a wealthy country in its comparatively low rates of payment for pensions and benefits. The real value of welfare benefits, including for unemployment, in the UK is unusually low for an advanced economy.

"Pensioner poverty is a significantly bigger problem in the UK than in Ireland. In the year 2019, pensioner poverty affected 15.5% of the UK population over age 66. The comparable figure for Ireland was 6.8%. In both the UK (including Northern Ireland) and Ireland the core state pension entitlement is related to the number of contributions made during a person's working life. But many people in both jurisdictions rely on means-tested pensions, because either they do not qualify for a contributions-based pension or that pension fails to meet their basic needs.

At the prevailing entitlement levels and exchange rates as of 2025, the Irish state pension for a single person (subject to contributions) is worth over £500 a year more than that in the UK (including Northern Ireland). However, at the time of the study 'Who is Better Off?', published in 2023, the gap was about £1,500 a year.

The ARINS study added: "Comparing the welfare benefits system North and South, the amounts payable and the period for which benefits are paid are complex and superficial analysis is unreliable. It is, though, notable that the devolved government in Northern Ireland spends more per capita on welfare support payments than the other UK administrations, with mitigations introduced to avoid some of the impacts of austerity imposed by the UK government and implemented in Great Britain. Despite this, support for people in deprivation tends to be greater in Ireland than in Northern Ireland or the rest of the UK."

The international crisis provoked by tariffs imposed by the United States may affect welfare and state pension payments in both Ireland and the UK, with cuts in the UK system already announced in response to its fiscal crisis.

CHAPTER SIX
REFORMING PUBLIC SERVICES ON AN ALL-ISLAND BASIS

Northern Ireland is arguably too small to provide a comprehensive health service for its citizens. Some health provision requires a larger size to support specialist consultants, who may need a sufficient through flow of patients to maintain and update their expertise and to justify the expenditure of the best technology. The larger the pool of patients within a system, the more scope there is to achieve the economies of scale required for an efficient health system.

This logic helps to explain why a unionist health minister – Edwin Poots – signed off significant all-island co-operation on health care. The Altnagelvin cancer care centre is used not only by patients in the Western Trust region, but also by those living in a different jurisdiction with a different model of health care in Co. Donegal. In return, Northern Ireland children needing heart surgery are treated in Dublin. This arrangement provides specialist care on the island, preventing the need for children to be air lifted to Great Britain for treatment – which could worsen their health condition and be distressing for parents because of travel difficulties and potential separation, with children sometimes needing to be in-patients for several weeks after surgery.

Another example is the Cooperation and Working Together (CAWT) project, a cross-border initiative dating from 1992 that addresses the specific problems encountered by patients in border areas. Its geography accounts for a quarter of the size of the island, covering a population of 1.6 million people. It adopts a pragmatic approach to resolving the needs of patients. Its functions have been supported by INTERREG funds of €36m. Its focus has included acute hospitals services and multiple adverse childhood experiences.[107]

The late Professor Jim Dornan argued that both Northern Ireland and the Irish Republic were below optimum size for a functioning, integrated and independent health system. Integration of the two systems – which might involve amalgamation, part amalgamation, partnerships or co-operation arrangements – would, he said, be the 'Goldilocks solution'. An all-island health service would be neither too small, nor too big.[108]

There are a number of opportunities in all-island health care partnerships, some of which have been referenced in the Irish government's Programme for Government of December 2024 and in earlier documents, including in relation to cancer care.

Ulster University's Professor Deirdre Heenan explained: "Over the past two decades health has been identified as a key area for increased cross-border working on the island of Ireland. To date though, the approach has been minimalist and often project specific. The global pandemic, the continuing fallout from Brexit and the establishment of the Shared Island initiative have pushed the broad issue of healthcare cooperation up the policy agenda.

"Theoretically, closer cooperation could deliver economies of scale, value for money, opportunities for clinical specialisation, and facilitate the sharing of knowledge. However, despite its obvious potential and policy significance, cross-border collaboration in healthcare has been the subject of remarkably little research attention." Funded by the Shared Island Unit, Professor Heenan conducted research into opportunities that exist for greater partnership.[109]

In her paper she wrote: "There are major structural and financial differences between the health systems in Northern Ireland and Ireland. However, they share similar core principles and values and face similar social, economic and political pressures. To a large extent the two systems have common core principles and have adopted similar approaches to tackling issues. Key challenges include an ageing and growing population, evolving healthcare needs, workforce planning, rising costs associated with medical technology and increasing expectations. With regard to access to primary care across Europe, both Ireland and Northern Ireland perform relatively poorly. The main causes of premature deaths are the same: cardiovascular disease, cancer, accidents and suicide."

In her study, Heenan quoted a former healthcare commissioner for Northern Ireland. "Healthcare should be housed in specialist centres; the cost of running multiple sites is colossal and actually delivers poor outcomes. We are a relatively small island with a small population and we simply can't support this model. Also, think of how recruitment could be revolutionised if we could attract and retain specialists from across the globe. Not just clinicians but administrators skilled in new technologies."

Both medical professionals and healthcare managers interviewed by Heenan stated their support for cross-border collaboration, while stressing this was not practically possible without support from political and organisational leadership. "A number of respondents suggested that any major initiative in healthcare on the island should be assessed against a number of agreed economic and healthcare objectives and this would help to ensure that services were aligned, and synergies identified in a systematic way."

Heenan concluded: "All-island approaches have the potential to address some of the current issues and ensure that Ireland as a whole is well placed to deal with future challenges. This joint approach involves both working within current structures and developing new all-island structures. Participants in this study were overwhelmingly positive about the opportunities presented by developing deeper and further integration. A consensus existed around an unassailable case for assessing key aspects of future healthcare provision through an all-island lens."

Policing is another area where cross-border co-operation is vital. Accordingly, the PSNI and the Garda have published a joint cross-border policing strategy.[110] Its four primary areas of focus are tackling crime and preventing harm; roads policing and road safety; community policing; and major emergency management.

A House of Commons Northern Ireland Affairs Committee report examined cross-border policing arrangements, which it concluded "are to the mutual benefit of all on these islands". The committee noted: "Over the past two decades, the PSNI and the Gardaí have made great progress in developing co-operation mechanisms to tackle cross-border criminality on the island of Ireland." The committee proposed various way in which the two police services can improve co-operation and the sharing of information and data.[111]

It is not only in health and policing where all-island solutions offer improved outcomes at lower cost. ESRI (the Economic and Social Research Institute) suggests there are opportunities for greater partnership within the education sector, providing advantages in both jurisdictions.

"In terms of North–South contact and co-operation, many stakeholders highlighted a few examples of very good practice. Across the stakeholder interviews, common examples included the areas of teacher education through SCoTENs (Standing Conference on Teacher Education North and South), strong links between the Inspectorates, the Middletown Centre for Autism, which is a joint North–South initiative, and the Joint Peace Fund. However, more generally, stakeholders highlighted that in many areas North– South links are ad hoc in nature and based on individual relationships or specific projects and initiatives, thus making sustained co-operation more challenging. Nonetheless, stakeholders reported a willingness to engage in cooperation around substantive issues.

"The fact that both jurisdictions face similar challenges in, among other factors, trying to counter educational disadvantage and create an inclusive educational system for students with special educational needs could provide a starting point for shared dialogue and learning."[112]

While there is some progress in various public services towards service co-operation, if not integration, environmental management is an area where there is far too little co-operation and engagement. One of the worst examples of this poor practice was with regard to the public inquiry into a proposed gold mine in the Sperrin mountains. The inquiry had to be suspended because Northern Ireland's Department for Infrastructure failed to meet its legal requirements to provide relevant information and notice to its counterparts in the Republic.[113]

Sadly this is not an isolated experience. While the environment and environmental protection is perhaps the most obvious application needing cross-border engagement (the environment does not recognise borders), it is one where there is a clear failure. "Almost all environmental challenges facing the island of Ireland – and there are many – will ultimately require cooperation across the border," states the Public Policy think-tank. "This has been recognised at government and policy level, and explicitly in the Good Friday/Belfast Agreement (GF/BA) where the environment is identified as a key area for cooperation. Despite this, Northern Ireland and Ireland have developed (with some exceptions) almost completely segregated environmental governance structures, legal and policy frameworks, and implementation processes."

Limited co-operation arrangements and legal frameworks that were in place while the UK was a member of the EU have been lost as a result of Brexit, further damaging the environment. "In addition to the governance implications of having two discrete sets of arrangements for protecting the environment on the island, meaningful cooperation in an advocacy context between environmental NGOs and civil society on the island has also been inhibited.

"Processes for civil society input, both at policy level and in the context of public participation in environmental decision-making, are generally separate and vary between the jurisdictions, making it harder for engagement on a cross-border basis. Concerns have been raised about the quality of (legally required) cross-border consultation, even on highly significant environmental plans and policies which will clearly impact the whole island. Funding streams and opportunities also differ, with relatively low incentives and only limited and relatively recent investment in work which transcends the political boundary. Navigating the differences between the two jurisdictions is therefore very complex for third sector organisations seeking to operate or collaborate to address serious environmental concerns across the island."[114]

The need for detailed cross-border engagement and co-operation in Ireland is obvious: it is unclear why in practice this is happening to such a limited extent. Given the environmental crisis in Northern Ireland as exemplified by pollution in Lough Neagh, Europe's largest illegal waste dump at Mobuoy in Derry and the counterproductive application of the Renewable Heat Incentive (which increased air pollution and the burning of wood pellets through a government subsidy scheme) it is reasonable to conclude that the environment is not a priority for Northern Ireland's politicians and other policy-makers.

CHAPTER SEVEN
THE SUBVENTION CONVERSATION

Northern Ireland's subvention is one of the most highly contested issues related to Irish unity. Strong arguments are put forward, asserting that the reality of the subvention is quite small, or, alternatively, that it is very large. Similarly, there are contrary arguments as to whether Irish unity would fairly quickly raise the North's income and quality of living, or whether the North would suffer from a stagnant economy that would severely damage the fiscal situation of the South.

Alongside those questions there sits a dispute over the effect of Brexit so far on Northern Ireland – which seems to have left the North in a less damaged position compared to that of Great Britain. (See Chapters Seven and Eight.) It is often suggested, as has Jonathan Powell, that the economy of the North is already moving towards greater convergence with the South into an all-island economy.

At its heart, the dispute revolves around the question of the extent to which the existing subvention as recognised by UK official statistics and Treasury budget documentation is the same, or even a similar, figure to the ongoing subvention Northern Ireland would require after it leaves the UK (if it does leave). The existing subvention includes figures that represent a proportional contribution towards UK national costs that will no longer be required if Northern Ireland leaves the UK. At its most obvious, this would include the Royal Family (a very small cost in the grand scheme of things).

Then there are items whose future costs are unclear – the armed services is an example of this. There would probably be no need for the North to pay into the UK Exchequer towards the British Army, but would Ireland's defence forces need to expand and, if so, by how much? Or would the new Irish state make a contribution to the UK in return for the British navy patrolling Irish waters? How can these matters be assessed today? Will Irish security costs for the army and Garda need to increase to deal with threats from loyalist paramilitaries? Both the UK and Ireland are likely to substantially increase their financial contributions to their armed services as a response to the Russia/Ukraine war and uncertainty over the security commitments of the United States under Trump. These factors are currently unquantifiable.

Other contentious and significant issues relate to any share of the ownership of UK national assets; distribution, if any, of UK national debts; and the liabilities for state pensions of people who gained entitlement from the UK state and paid into the scheme, but similarly those with entitlement to UK public sector pensions. These questions are subject to different views as are explained here.

At the foundation of the Northern Ireland state, there was no subvention from the British taxpayer towards Northern Ireland according to Professor John Doyle. He writes: "When Northern Ireland was created it ran a government surplus and paid an annual 'Imperial Contribution' to the British government. However, as the economy declined, from the late 1920s onwards, the level of this payment fell and by 1938 the UK government was subsidising the cost of public services in Northern Ireland."

A different perspective is suggested by Professor John FitzGerald and Professor Edgar Morgenroth, referencing research by Esmond Birnie of Ulster University. "Since its establishment as a separate regime in 1921, Northern Ireland has received significant support from central Government to provide services within Northern Ireland."[115]

Irrespective of whether the subvention began at the birth of Northern Ireland or a short number of years later, at the time of its establishment Northern Ireland was regarded as industrially successful. Northern Ireland was the location of a strong manufacturing sector based on the shipbuilding and linen industries, providing the North with a much more prosperous outlook than the South at the point of their creation. This was not the result of partition, but partition did create economic difficulties for both jurisdictions, which experienced dislocation of pre-existing supply chains.[116]

The context for partition included significant population decline. John Bradley describes a 55% decline in population between 1841 and 1951 in the area that became the Irish Republic. Notably, by 1911 the population of Belfast (386,947) was larger than that of Dublin (304,802). Today the population of Dublin is nearly twice that of 1911, whereas that of Belfast has declined.[117]

In the period following the 1920s, the industrial sectors on which the North's economy was dependent became more challenging and the subvention increased substantially over the years. FitzGerald has suggested that the onset of the 1929 depression was the factor that initiated the subvention for Northern Ireland. This was followed by a long period of economic stagnation[118], before a significant worsening of the economic position of Northern Ireland as the Troubles took hold in the 1960s.

Fionnuala McKenna and Martin Melaugh explain: "The subvention from Britain to Northern Ireland was £3,340 million in 1995-96. The subvention represents the shortfall between the total amount of money that is raised in Northern Ireland, mainly in taxation, and the total amount spent in the region, mainly on public services and security. The subvention grew steadily over the period from 1970 to 1996."[119]

The Office for National Statistics calculates that the net fiscal balance (ie subvention) for Northern Ireland for the 2022/23 fiscal year (the most recent year published) was a deficit of £14.5bn.[120] ESRI analysis concludes that government expenditure per capita in Northern Ireland is €27,471 a year, compared to €16,404 tax receipts per person. By contrast the figures for the Republic are €22,279 per capita for expenditure and €27,970 in tax receipts per person. The ratio of capital spend, a determinant of economic performance, is reversed, with 8.7% of Northern Ireland expenditure used for capital projects, against 13.4% in the Republic.[121]

Northern Ireland's nominal subvention from the UK government has increased by a significant level in recent years. The following chart from FitzGerald and Morgenroth explains the increase in terms of percentage of Northern Ireland GDP.

Figure 1: Northern Ireland Subvention from Central Government as % of Northern Ireland GDP

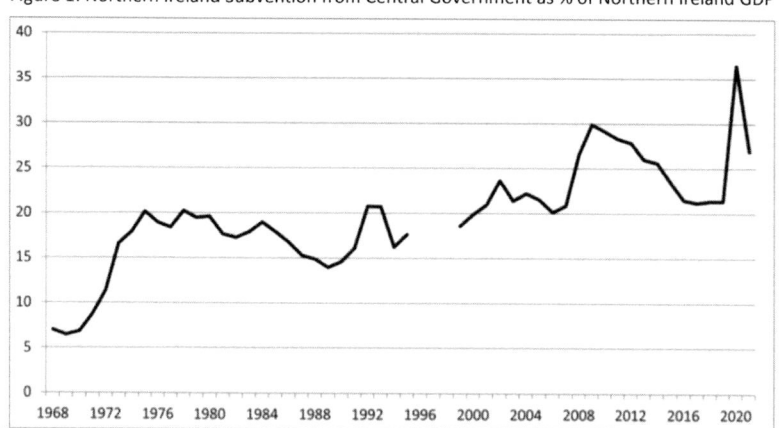

Source: John FitzGerald and Edgar Morgenroth, reproduced with permission

This chart makes clear that there have been three separate substantial rises in the subvention, measured as percentages of GDP. The early 1970s obviously coincides with the worst period of the Troubles. This led to a very large increase in security spending by the UK state and local agencies, as well as a collapse in the economy and related falls in tax revenues and increased social security costs. (There was a 41% drop in externally owned manufacturing facilities between 1973 and 1990.[122]) The second big increase, from 2008, was the period in which the global economy suffered very severely, afflicting Northern Ireland along with other places. Recovery can be seen to be slow. The third big rise was related to the costs of addressing the Covid pandemic.

It is reasonable to make additional observations in relation to these subvention costs. One is that the 1998 GFA did not lead – as many expected – to a substantial improvement in the North's economy and therefore a fall in the subvention. To the contrary, the subvention continued to rise. Indeed, it has been suggested (perhaps mischievously) that while the GFA led to the expected Peace Dividend, this was actually delivered to the South rather than the North. Others – led by Graham Brownlow[123] – have concluded that the GFA provided a small economic Peace Dividend. The real benefit has been social, in particular the fall in killings, rather than economic.

The leading academic arguing against the proposition that the size of the UK subvention to Northern Ireland makes Irish unity unaffordable for the Republic is Professor John Doyle, who is Vice President for Research at Dublin City University. "The figure of £10bn, frequently quoted as representing the UK government annual subvention to Northern Ireland, is a UK accounting exercise," argues Doyle. "The total includes central UK government costs allocated to Northern Ireland that would not be relevant to a United Ireland."[124] Doyle suggests that as well as defence expenditure, other existing items included in the calculated subvention figure that would not transfer under Irish unity include UK national debt repayments and pension liabilities. He also believes that calculations of Northern Ireland's share of UK tax revenues are underestimated. Moreover, he asserts that unity would lead to the North adopting the South's economic model, providing a positive impact on economic growth and tax revenues. "The underlying economy, taxation system and the type of public services that are provided in health, welfare, education and infrastructure, will be the real issues that will shape the costs and benefits of a united Ireland."

Doyle explains (and this is a generally agreed point) that at its creation, the Northern Ireland economy was a manufacturing powerhouse, which generated more tax revenues than were spent there. This began to change in the late 1920s, with a subvention being required by 1938, initially at a modest level. This rose as unemployment increased. He adds that "by the 1950s the economy was significantly dependent on a subvention from London". There was a significant subvention even before the advent of the Troubles.

Doyle continues: "The economic cost of the Covid-19 pandemic will see a significant one-off increase in the subvention, but it is the scale and composition of the underlying deficit that is relevant to the debate on the political future of the island. There is a broad consensus that Northern Ireland's economy is very weak, that this weakness predated the modern conflict and also that the economic growth that was expected after the 1998 Good Friday Agreement has been very modest." As a result of Brexit, EU funding to Northern Ireland that had been worth 8.4% of its GDP was lost.

While the Northern Ireland economy is weak, it is normal in any country to be comprised of regions / nations that have stronger and weaker economies. "Like Northern Ireland, Scotland and Wales also run deficits as would most regions in England if they had devolved government. For Northern Ireland the difference is that the published deficit is large, by comparison, and the debate surrounding it is politically charged. Focusing on the subvention is seen by some unionists as a critique of Northern Ireland redolent of Charles Haughey's famous phrase a 'failed political entity'. To overcome this, the 2016 Ulster Unionist Party manifesto highlighted that Northern Ireland did not always require a subvention, choosing to emphasise Northern Ireland's ability to improve economically, rather than acknowledging the level of support from Britain. In contrast, supporters of a united Ireland see the calculation of the subvention as exaggerated and part of a 'project fear' campaign by British Conservatives—similar in style to the 2014 campaign against Scottish independence."

Doyle goes on: "Northern Ireland's economy is weak, and levels of poverty are high, compared to either Ireland or other regions of the UK. As the economy in the Irish republic developed over the past quarter century, Northern Ireland's has remained by comparison stagnant. The subvention is a symptom of this weakness, but it is incorrect to assume that it would simply transfer in its totality to a united Ireland. Understanding how the UK state calculates the subvention is therefore essential to analysing what parts of it would be relevant to a united Ireland."

The crux of Doyle's argument is not to challenge the calculation of the existing subvention, but rather to argue that this subvention does not represent a subsidy that the Irish government would be required to meet as a result of Irish unity. "The figure of £10bn for the Northern Ireland subvention, so often quoted in the media, is not an estimate of the deficit that would exist on day one of a united Ireland, even though it is frequently used as though it is. It is not calculated by the UK Office for National Statistics for that purpose. The UK Office for National Statistics publishes a figure annually as part of its Net Public Balances Report (NPBR) and its most recent report stated that the gap between revenue raised in Northern Ireland and public expenditure in Northern Ireland, plus an allocation to Northern Ireland of a share of central UK public expenditure, is just under £9.4bn for the year ended 2019."

Much of the calculations behind the subvention figures are estimates that cannot be firmly grounded. "Determining what revenue is raised in Northern Ireland and what public expenditure should be allocated to Northern Ireland is not a simple task and the ONS acknowledge that different methodologies will give different results . . . . Taking the issue of taxation first, some elements of the estimation of revenue raised in Northern Ireland are relatively straightforward. For example, income tax and domestic rates paid by individuals who are resident there, and VAT and business taxes for firms based exclusively in Northern Ireland. However, many other taxes can only be estimated. VAT, Capital Gains Tax and corporation taxes paid by companies with activities throughout the UK are almost always paid through their head office address, and there is a significant bias towards London as the HQ of so many companies. It is not possible to tell from business' VAT returns how much VAT has been paid in a given region. Likewise, the share of corporation tax 'earned' in different regions can only be estimated."

Doyle points out that NICVA has previously complained that estimates for the generation of business taxes in Northern Ireland are particularly weakly evidenced. Moreover, much of Northern Ireland's nominal share of UK costs are not related to actual expenditure in Northern Ireland and therefore provides no basis for assuming what future costs related to Northern Ireland would be post Irish unity.

Significantly, some costs would have to be negotiated between the two governments – either before or after a referendum. These negotiations would relate both to the total sums involved and also any possible timetable for transferring agreed revenue and capital costs. Pensions is "one of the biggest issues". Given the importance of this matter, Doyle's analysis is included here at length.

In the year for 2018, these cost £3.438bn in relation to Northern Ireland. "This is the comprehensive cost of pensions benefits, paid to people whose address is in Northern Ireland, and it includes both public occupational pensions that are not covered by a separate pension fund, and means-tested pensions. This cost of pensions would be unlikely to transfer to a united Ireland.

"At present, the UK pays pensions to people who have worked some or all of their lives in the UK, but now live elsewhere. Many Irish citizens, in retirement in Ireland, receive their UK pension seamlessly, and the two tax and social welfare systems have a well-developed model of cooperation. It seems consistent that the UK would pay pension liability that had been built up, based on individuals' tax and social insurance contributions or caring responsibilities, during Northern Ireland's membership of the United Kingdom, leaving the new Irish state to take over liability building up from the date of the creation of the new state.

"Accepting liability for pensions built up while working in the UK would also be consistent with the approach taken during the UK's withdrawal from the EU. Like Ireland, all social welfare-based pensions and most public sector employment-based pensions are paid from general taxation and not from a legally separated fund. However, there is a strong sense of pension 'entitlement' in both Ireland and the UK, notwithstanding the absence of legally separate pension funds.

"While the UK could reject any obligation to pay such pensions, a refusal to acknowledge lifelong contributions through social insurance (or equivalent caring responsibilities) would lead to very inconsistent outcomes. A person who worked in the UK, and retired to Dublin or Spain, would get a UK pension, in the current practice, but if they lived and stayed in Northern Ireland they might not. If people had worked for some of their life in Britain and some in Northern Ireland, how would their contributions be divided up as between the years spent working in Northern Ireland compared to in Britain? There is no further breakdown of these pension costs, between for example means-tested and 'contributory' pensions, or between the cost of direct cash payments versus other pension-related benefits.

"While pensions will be a matter for bi-lateral negotiation between the two governments, it is consistent with other practice that the UK would accept such obligations, which had been built up through tax and social insurance contributions, and caring responsibilities up to the date of Northern Ireland leaving the UK, while a united Ireland would take over such future liabilities building up from day one of the new state. This is also the most likely manner in which the UK would cover a transitional (and by definition annually declining) financial contribution to Northern Ireland, post-unity."

By contrast to Doyle, Professor John FitzGerald (and others) argue that the UK would be under no obligation to pay state pensions to its former citizens then living in a united Ireland. FitzGerald points out that national insurance contributions were used to meet the costs of existing pensioners, not to build up a fund for contributors' own pensions. On that basis, there is no fund to meet the costs of current and future pensions, so meeting the costs of those pensions would fall on the new united Ireland's state. Those who disagree argue that irrespective of how the contributions were used, the contributions created a liability on the British government to meet the cost of state pensions. (Public sector pensions create a separate issue. Contributions in some of these schemes went into funds that were invested to meet the costs of future pensions. But others, such as the NHS and teachers' pensions, like the state pension, were not invested into funded schemes.)

The next most significant question in relation to the subvention is Northern Ireland's share of the UK public debt. This is calculated in the existing subvention on the basis of the proportionate share of the debt, based on the size of the population.

Doyle continues: "This debt is the legal responsibility of the UK, and any agreement from the government of Ireland to take over some of the debt could only be agreed voluntarily, as part of a wider transitional package . . . . In the historic case of the creation of the Irish Free State, the allocated share of UK debt was written off in 1925 when the Free State accepted the boundary commission report, which the UK regarded as the finalisation of the transition from the point of view of UK law. In the event of a vote to create a United Ireland, Northern Ireland would be leaving the UK in accordance with the provisions of UK law, and therefore the Free State precedent is relevant. In comparable international cases, assets as well as liabilities were distributed between two successor states, and the political context for these negotiations has been important. International precedent suggests that if in negotiations during transition, the UK government pushed to have Ireland take over a share of UK debt, Ireland would then be entitled to a proportionate share of UK assets outside Northern Ireland—both national institutions based throughout the UK, and embassy and state properties outside UK territory.

"While it is possible to value Northern Ireland's share of UK assets outside Northern Ireland, it is more probable that some form of stand-still agreement would be reached, whereby the new united Ireland would waive its rights to a share of UK 'national' property, outside Northern Ireland, and of UK assets abroad, and in return the UK would not seek to transfer a proportion of the UK national debt to a united Ireland. ONS data gives a figure of £1.6bn as Northern Ireland's 2019 contribution to interest on the UK national debt."

The existing subvention also includes moneys allocated as unidentifiable expenditure and accounting adjustments, which includes depreciation and VAT refunds. "The report for the Irish Oireachtas compiled by Mark Daly chose to exclude accounting adjustments in their entirety on the basis that they do not represent actual expenditure, which a new state would need to find on day one." Doyle calculates that once these amendments are made to the subvention figure then the potential subvention from the Republic of Ireland to accommodate Northern Ireland would be around £2.4bn, or €2.8bn. This is "within a range that a future state could cope with on a transitional basis", concludes Doyle. In addition, there could be transitional support from the European Union and possibly the United States. "The precise 'subvention' will be subject to the negotiations between the Irish and British governments."[125]

The Irish government has itself calculated the Northern Ireland fiscal deficit, which – for the 2019-20 year – comes out at slightly over £7bn, once non-Northern Ireland expenditure is stripped out.[126]

FitzGerald and Morgenroth make substantially different assumptions and arguments in their calculations of the existing subvention and the likely cost to the Irish government of absorbing Northern Ireland into the Irish state. They do, though, make the same point that some of the terms of separation and the costs are unsure and will be determined by negotiation between the two governments.

TABLE 2

Northern Ireland Public Finances summary (£ million)	2019/20
Totally managed expenditure (TME)	30,118
Minus accounting adjustments	4,106
Equals total expenditure on services	26,012
Of which: identifiable expenditure	22,699
Of which: non-identifiable expenditure	3,313
Tax revenue raised in Northern Ireland	15,668
Other revenues	4,149
Total revenue	19,817
Fiscal deficit (TME minus total revenue)	10,301
NI-specific fiscal gap	7,031
(NI tax revenue minus identifiable expenditure)	

Source: Shared Island, Shared Economy, Ireland's Department of Finance[127]

TABLE 3

Recalculated subvention to reflect those elements relevant to a United Ireland As calculated by Professor John Doyle (£ million)

Northern Ireland deficit as per Office for National Statistics, 2019	9,367
Removing from this as not relevant to a United Ireland:	
UK pensions	3,438
Allocated UK debt charges	1,600
UK defence allocation (less 20% for RoI increase)	925
Tax underestimate related to London HQ impact	500
Outside of UK expenditure	500
Total adjustments for subvention in relation to a UI	6,963
Remaining subvention prior to policy decisions	2,404

Source: John Doyle[128]

FitzGerald and Morgenroth say: "The precise terms under which Northern Ireland could leave the UK would be subject to negotiation. In the case of Ireland's exit from the UK in 1922, it accepted a share of the UK debt at the time of departure. If Scotland had left the UK in 2014, it too would have taken its share of the UK debt. This reflects the fact that it is normal when a country breaks up in a negotiated manner that assets and liabilities are shared among the two new jurisdictions. This also happened in the case of the break-up of the US state of Virginia in the 1860s and, more recently, the break-up of the USSR and of Czechoslovakia in the early 1990s.

"Some commentators have suggested that in a negotiated settlement, the UK would agree to waive this debt liability for Northern Ireland in return for the ending of the fiscal transfer to Northern Ireland. However, if Scotland had voted for independence in 2014, the agreement for the break-up of the UK would have entailed Scotland leaving it with a share of the UK debt. This is likely to set a precedent for any eventual departures from the UK, whether it is Scotland or Northern Ireland. To allow successive regions of the UK to depart leaving all of the debt to be serviced by the remaining population in the UK would seem difficult to justify."

Similarly, in relation to pension liabilities, FitzGerald and Morgenroth make a more conservative or negative interpretation of obligations. "Bergin and McGuinness, 2020, argue that, because the old age pension in Northern Ireland is paid to those who have contributed over their lifetime through social insurance, the insurance-based pension would constitute an existing liability of the UK at departure. However, this ignores the fact that the pension scheme is run on a pay-as-you-go basis rather than a funded basis. The social insurance pensions paid out in the UK are generally equal to the insurance contributions paid in each year. The idea that the UK would continue to pay pensions while a united Ireland collected the related social insurance contributions seems most improbable. If people from Northern Ireland moved to Great Britain after unification they would, of course, be entitled to a pension there when they reached retirement age.

"There is currently an agreement between the UK and Ireland which provides for workers moving between jurisdictions being able to rely on their combined insurance contributions in qualifying for pensions. This agreement reflects a need to provide for labour mobility between the two jurisdictions. However, a new agreement would be needed under the changed terms of a unified Ireland and, for the reasons given above, it is unlikely that the UK would continue to pay pensions to people in Northern Ireland. When Ireland became independent in 1922, there was never any question of the UK having a liability after independence to the then social insurance scheme, which covered unemployment rather than pensions. It was funded on a pay-as-you-go basis."

Moreover, FitzGerald and Morgenroth suggest that the process by which a referendum on reunification would be held places the Irish government in a weak position of negotiation with the British. "The process by which unification would come about would first involve a referendum in Northern Ireland. If the North voted for unification, then Ireland would have to agree the precise terms of a new constitution, specifying in detail the institutions of the new united Ireland. In turn, this would have to be voted on by Ireland. If that constitution were accepted by the people of Ireland, then a final settlement would have to be agreed with the UK. However, having decided irrevocably on unification, the Irish side would be in a very weak negotiating position. Thus, any concessions on the debt and pensions should not be counted on and they would not be clear until after a final settlement was agreed between a united Ireland and the UK."

(It is for these, and other, reasons that the book 'A New Ireland' suggested a two-stage referendum, to avoid a Brexit type situation where voters were unaware of the detail of what they voted for. We proposed a two-stage referendum – one of principle and a second after the negotiations. Leo Varadkar has proposed similar. However, Professor Brendan O'Leary has argued that such an approach is not possible as it is inconsistent with the Good Friday Agreement.)

FitzGerald and Morgenroth also disagree with Doyle in relation to the speed and likelihood of the North becoming economically aligned with the South and, therefore, the likely increase in tax revenues in a manner that would reduce the subvention.

They say "While the very low productivity of Northern Ireland's economy continues to leave it among the poorest regions in the UK, it will have a very large fiscal deficit. Even though Ireland has a much higher national income, funding the needs of the people of Northern Ireland in a united Ireland would put huge financial pressure on the people of Ireland, resulting in an immediate major reduction in their living standards.

"If, instead, Northern Ireland made major changes in its economy designed to dramatically raise productivity, over time this would narrow the gap in living standards between Northern Ireland, the rest of the UK and Ireland. In turn, this would reduce the Northern Ireland deficit and also reduce the cost of applying similar standards in Northern Ireland to those in Ireland. This could substantially reduce the cost of unification.

"If Northern Ireland chose to remain in the UK indefinitely, by reforming its economy it would also greatly enhance its economic position within the UK, realising a substantial improvement in its relative standard of living. However, even under the most favourable circumstances with optimal policies, it is likely to be at least two decades before the productivity gap could be substantially narrowed. Nonetheless, the sooner such changes are implemented, the sooner the benefits will accrue to the people of Northern Ireland whether they remain in the UK or eventually join in a united Ireland."

In a presentation to the Joint Oireachtas Committee on the Implementation of the Good Friday Agreement 23 May 2024, Professor John Doyle rejected the calculations and assessments made by Professor John FitzGerald and Professor Edgar Morgenroth in their joint IIEA paper, in which they concluded that the initial costs of a United Ireland would be €20bn pa over 20 years. He argued that their assessments were "wildly inaccurate as the report contains significant errors and is based on entirely unreasonable assumptions".

Doyle suggested that it was wrong to expect public sector wages to immediately match those of the South, while not recognising the associated increased tax revenues and pension contributions. He noted that German reunification had involved merging salary levels over a

30 year period and posited a 15 year transition period as being an affordable option. Doyle disputed the use of a £10bn annual subvention as a starting point for calculations and challenged assumptions on pension liabilities and increasing costs. "It is not believable that the Government of a united Ireland would agree to be left with liability for both debt and pensions," said Doyle.

Further, he argued that the North's economy and tax revenues would grow through unification: "an increase in the underlying growth rate in NI, of 2% above recent long term patterns would see the costs of transition covered and the fiscal deficit ended in approximately 10 years, after which NI would run a surplus. In this case, the level of transition costs can be covered by the Irish state, through a modest increase in borrowing or taxation. Current tax revenues are approximately €88bn in the Republic and €22bn in Northern Ireland. A requirement to raise €2.5bn per annum to deal with an underlying deficit and provide some additional resources for public services, this would represent a borrowing requirement of three quarters of one per cent of the GNI of a united Ireland – or an increase in taxation revenues (based on economic growth or tax changes) of just over 2%, for those transitional ten years."

The debate on the size of the existing and future subvention is not merely a two way disagreement between Doyle on the one hand and FitzGerald and Morgenroth on the other. Esmond Birnie of Ulster University (and previously an MLA for the Ulster Unionist Party) has made similar arguments to those of FitzGerald and Morgenroth.[129] Seamus McGuinness and Adele Bergin of the Economic and Social Research Institute are more optimistic about the impact of Irish unity on the North's productivity and therefore believe the future size of subvention will be less than that suggested by FitzGerald and Morgenroth. They also suggest that the 13 year handover period of Hong Kong to China provides an indication for the timetable for Irish unity.

They explain: "Arguably, a negotiated transition period would allow both the UK and Irish governments' an opportunity to co-ordinate policy to allow for a gradual re-integration which should also involve the introduction of new education, regional and industrial policies aimed at increasing productivity levels in NI. Furthermore ... Irish re-unification will also involve NI re-entering the EU, which opens the possibility of EU involvement in the transition process. In summary, it is extremely difficult to be definitive around the costs of re-unification to the RoI tax payer, as this will be dependent upon a number of unknowns including negotiations around debt interest, the length of any transition period, the relative role and contributions of the UK, RoI and EU in managing such a transition and the success of any policies aimed at improving NI productivity levels."[130]

A study by the Irish government's Department of Social Protection has calculated that if on day one of a unified Irish state the new government uplifted all welfare payments in the North to the same level of entitlement as in the South, this would cost the new government €22bn a year.[131]

It is suggested by FitzGerald and Morgenroth that the situation in relation to existing UK liabilities, such as pensions, will follow the precedent agreed between the Scottish and UK governments in relation to its 2014 referendum. The Scottish government, under the SNP, agreed to take over responsibility for state pensions from the British government. However, it is unclear whether that responsibility included the Scottish government accepting all financial liabilities, or whether it expected the British government to provide a financial settlement to recognise its outstanding liabilities.

"Future Scottish governments would be responsible for the pensions system in an independent Scotland. Responsibility for paying for state pensions would rest with the Scottish Government. All accrued state and public service pension rights and entitlements would be honoured and protected, and state and public service pensions would continue to be paid on time and in full."[132] In addition, according to details of the agreement published by the British government, "Some proportion of the liabilities for public service pension schemes would also become the responsibility of an independent Scottish state, with estimates suggesting the total liability figure could be in the region of £100bn."[133]

In its White Paper, prior to the referendum, the Scottish Government stated: "The financial position that Scotland will inherit upon independence will depend in part on negotiations between the Scottish and Westminster Governments following a Yes vote. For example, the proportion of UK public sector debt which an independent Scotland will assume responsibility for." This suggested that net debt might be apportioned by reference to the balance of public spending and taxation since 1980/81, or alternatively based on the population share.

A significant difference between Scotland and Northern Ireland is that the Scottish government believed it was negotiating from a position of financial strength, with projections for continued large revenues from offshore oil reserves.

The UK state's fiscal crisis is likely to make its financing of Northern Ireland and other devolved nations and regions increasingly difficult to sustain. Economist David McWilliams has gone so far as to suggest that the UK may need to go to the IMF to provide support for its debt, with the international markets increasingly concerned about its fiscal position.[134] Whether the crisis goes as far as that or not, the subvention question is not merely about whether the Republic can afford the North, but also about whether the UK can do so or wants to. This, in turn, is dependent on internal UK – specifically English – politics, which appears to be in a state of flux or uncertainty.

CHAPTER EIGHT
THE BREXIT EFFECT

It is widely accepted that Brexit has damaged the UK economically, as well as left it politically isolated. The UK government's heavily criticised 2024 Budget increased employers' national insurance levy, raising £36bn, a smaller amount than the tax revenues, £40bn, foregone as a result of the Brexit effect. However, it would be misleading to suggest that the 2024 Budget was a straight correction of the lost revenues caused by Brexit – the previous government had already done that during a Parliamentary term when tax revenues increased to a then record high.[135]

"The Brexit hit has inevitably led to tax rises, because a slower-growing economy requires higher taxation to fund public services and benefits. If Brexit had not happened, most of the tax rises that then Chancellor Rishi Sunak announced in March 2022 would not have been necessary. If the UK economy had grown in line with the doppelgänger [the economy that would have been, had the UK stayed in the EU], tax revenues would have been around £40bn higher on an annual basis (if we apply the same tax-to-GDP ratio as in 2021-2 – 34%)."[136]

The Office for Budget Responsibility is the official body that monitors the British government's fiscal planning. It, too, recognises the economic damage caused by Brexit. It states: "The post-Brexit trading relationship between the UK and EU, as set out in the 'Trade and Cooperation Agreement' (TCA) that came into effect on 1 January 2021, will reduce long-run productivity by 4% relative to remaining in the EU. This largely reflects our view that the increase in non-tariff barriers on UK-EU trade acts as an additional impediment to the exploitation of comparative advantage . . . . Both exports and imports will be around 15% lower in the long run than if the UK had remained in the EU . . . . New trade deals with non-EU countries will not have a material impact, and any effect will be gradual."

Ironically, given the debate prior to the referendum, the OBR no longer believes that leaving the EU will reduce net inward migration. It has "revised up our projections for net migration to reflect evidence of sustained strength in inward migration since the post-Brexit migration regime was introduced. We now assume net migration settles at 315,000 a year in the medium term." This reflects the increase in non-EU inward migration.

While a minority of economists continue to argue that Brexit has not damaged the UK economy[137], there is something approaching a consensus not just among economists, but also amongst the public that the impact has been seriously negative. "Two-thirds of the British public think Brexit has damaged the economy, while even among Leave voters only one in five think the impact has been positive," writes Jonathan Portes.[138]

Analysis from NIESR goes further: "The United Kingdom has experienced slower economic growth following the global financial crisis and its exit from the European Union. Our estimates suggest that had the post-2010 trends been sustained, real income and private consumption per capita could have been 8-9% and 11-12% higher than current figures, respectively."[139]

However, this might overstate the impact of Brexit. Leaving the EU happened in similar time to Covid and the Russia-Ukraine war, which were also damaging. And economic growth after the 2008 crash was faster than at normal times. Moreover, it is generally recognised by economists that George Osborne's austerity controls lessened economic growth in following years by reducing investment in the factors that lead to improved productivity, including education and skills, as well as damaging the health of the nation and its workforce.[140]

Despite this, the evidence is very clear that Brexit has seriously damaged UK trade and tax revenues. Moreover, as tax revenues have increased so has the underlying economy become more damaged as it reduces available business capital for investment. It becomes a downward spiral.

Just as significant is the political isolation caused by Brexit. The potential damage caused by Brexit on the small Irish economy was mitigated, and to a large extent prevented, through Ireland's membership of the European Union. The UK is no longer part of a larger grouping of countries able to provide mutual protection from the largest external economies of the United States and China.

The United Kingdom has made itself diplomatically isolated at a time when the United States has entered its most volatile period in modern history. It remains unclear at the time of writing what Donald Trump intends to do over the longer term with regard to trade barriers and tariffs, but the EU has size on its size and a greater capacity than has the UK in terms of retaliation and mutual trade.

However, should Trump impose tariffs on one of the EU or the UK and not the other and consequently Northern Ireland finds itself in the worst of the two tariff regimes, this is likely to create a new political crisis in the North. How tariffs would work for Northern Ireland as constitutionally part of the UK but within the EU's Single Market for trade is not, as yet, clear.

Brexit has had a significant impact on Northern Ireland's politics, leading to a significant increase in support for Irish unity. Amongst those who voted 'remain' in the referendum in Northern Ireland, only 37% believe it should continue to be part of the UK. Prior to the vote, 64% of that group did.[141]

CHAPTER NINE
THE ALL-ISLAND ECONOMY

ESRI – Ireland's Economic and Social Research Institute – has provided the context for this conversation. "Northern Ireland occupies a unique position following Brexit and the Windsor Framework. It is part of the UK fiscal, welfare and monetary unions – where the main policy levers are mostly exercised at a UK national level – along with its national economic policies for devolved administrations and regions. Simultaneously, it remains within the EU Single Market for goods with Dual EU/UK regulatory regimes, participates in the Common Travel Area (CTA) between the United Kingdom and Ireland and is supported by a commitment to continue specified areas of North-South cooperation. The economic effects of this will continue to evolve over time. Whatever the background situation, it is clear that the economies of both Northern Ireland and Ireland can have a mutually beneficial impact on each other through improved economic outcomes on both sides of the border and enhanced interaction."[142]

The value of cross-border trade in Ireland has substantially increased since Brexit. Total trade in goods and services in 2023 was €14.3bn (£12.4bn), up 26% from 2022, and rising further in 2024.[143] The majority of this was in goods, which rose 30% from 2022, to €11.3bn / £9.8bn. These figures reflect, in part, difficulties in East-West trade resulting from Brexit and the sometimes smoother flow of trade cross-border. Brexit has also changed the focus of some Northern Ireland business leaders, who are now more interested in the South and the rest of the EU than what has become a smaller more isolated market of Great Britain outside of the EU and subject to some regulatory divergence.

The Irish Times reports – using official statistics – that cross-border trade has grown from €2bn a year in 1998, when the GFA was signed, to over €15bn now. Sales South to North have grown 60% in the last decade, while those North to South have jumped 90%.[144]

A report from the Irish government helpfully presented the significant rise in all-island trade in a graph, demonstrating that while RoI-NI services have risen slightly in the period 2011 to 2022, those relating to NI-RoI services and RoI-NI goods rose significantly, the increase in NI-RoI goods trade has increased dramatically, rising from just over €3bn to around €5.5bn.[145]

It is worth referring again to the observation from Jonathan Powell, Tony Blair's chief negotiator in the period leading to the Good Friday Agreement, on the relationship between all-island economic connections and the future political relationships. As we noted in the introduction, Powell suggested Irish unity post-Brexit was increasingly likely. "In Northern Ireland, once you put a border between Northern Ireland and the rest of the United Kingdom, Northern Ireland is going to be part of a united Ireland for economic purposes, that will increase the tendency for a united Ireland for political reasons too."[146]

It is interesting to observe conflicting views of the impact of Brexit and the continued stronger commercial links between Northern Ireland and the EU. Some unionists suggest that the fundamentals are unchanged, with talk of the all-island economy being overhyped. Jim Allister MP said: "the growth area of the Northern Ireland economy is the services sector, which is the one sector not included by the protocol—it is outside all that. The one sector that is outside the protocol is increasing. There is a clear message in that."[147] Gavin Robinson MP added, in the same House of Commons debate: "Invest Northern Ireland, the body charged with encouraging foreign direct investment into Northern Ireland and with growing our economy, cannot point to one example of business investing in Northern Ireland as a direct result of the Windsor framework."[148]

By contrast, a report from the Irish government focusing on the flow of trade states: "Goods trade between Ireland and Northern Ireland has grown substantially since the exit of Great Britain from the EU's Single Market and Customs Union. The unique status of Northern Ireland with its access to both the EU and UK markets has driven a recent increase in cross-border trade and potentially may feed into broader economic linkages across the island. As exporting firms have better outcomes across a range of key indicators, including employment and productivity, expanding participation in exporting can make an important contribution to the broader performance of an economy."[149]

However, it is important that in reporting on all-island trade, a misleading picture is not created. Great Britain remains Northern Ireland's most significant external market, still much larger than that of the Republic of Ireland. At the same time, it must be recognised that Ireland is the second largest export market, with a growing share of trade. It should also be noted that Ireland is a much more important export market for Northern Ireland, than Northern Ireland is for the Republic. It can be seen that Northern Ireland is more dependent on Great Britain for imports than for export, whereas it sells substantially more to the Republic than it imports.[150]

TABLE 4

Top 10 destinations and origins of total trade, percentage share, 2021

Northern Ireland	Imports	Exports	Ireland	Imports	Exports
Great Britain	65.49	46.58	U.S.	17.01	31
Ireland	11.93	28.58	Great Britain	14.15	8.84
Germany	1.88	8.1	Germany	7.97	11
U.S.	3.22	1.78	China	7.12	7.5
China	2.81	1.08	France	10.61	3.29
Netherlands	1.74	1.52	Belgium	3.76	8.44
France	0.83	1.99	Netherlands	5.63	5.83
Belgium	1.17	1.31	N. Ireland	4.71	2.29
Spain	0.51	1.27	Switzerland	4.87	1.75
Italy	0.87	0.87	Italy	2.07	2.71
Rest of EU	9.52	18.03	Rest of EU	37.35	37.91

Source: Shared Island, Shared Economy, Ireland's Department of Finance[151]

As well as trade, there is also an all-island labour market, though at present this is significantly hampered by differences in tax treatments and also benefits and pension rules between the two jurisdictions. As a study by the Centre for Cross-Border Cooperation observes: "The current rules and regulations, and their practical application, need to be assessed to ensure that they do in fact support the free movement of workers between the jurisdictions. Further, the ability of non-Irish and non-UK residents to work on a cross-border basis will also be a critical consideration in what constitutes the all-island labour market going forward."[152]

Despite this, there are assessed as being 10,541 daily journeys North to South for work and 7,777 South to North work journeys. The greater number of commutes North to South is reflective of the higher pay in the South, though in the North West the main commuter flow is into Northern Ireland because of the availability of public sector jobs.[153] University, college and school students also commute across the border. At least 30,000 people cross the border daily for work or study.[154]

It is clear that the all-island economy is growing significantly, but without it being the most important economic connection for either the North (which is Great Britain) or the South (which is the United States).

It is recognised by big business that greater co-operation and integration of the Southern and Northern economies have the potential to benefit the whole island. IBEC and the CBI jointly stated: "Many aspects of the All-Island economy have performed strongly despite the challenges of Brexit but there are a number of areas which would benefit from further cooperation. In particular, it is clear to business leaders that there is an urgent need to progress North-South policy coordination to protect the Single Electricity Market, secure the island's energy supply and meet legally mandated net zero climate action goals. There is also a need to address obstacles to cross-border working to take full advantage of the All-Island labour market."[155]

Angela McGowan, Director, CBI Northern Ireland, added: "The business community want to see good collaboration both North-South and East-West. Firms are hungry to reap all the potential advantages that a well-developed All-Island economy can deliver. These advantages include: a bigger market for sales and supply chains, a greater labour market pool, improved connectivity for trade, tourists and workers as well as access to a secure supply of cheaper green energy. By working together, we are much more likely to deliver that economic prize."

A number of steps are required to further strengthen the all-island economy. These include:

- Harmonisation of tax, benefits and pensions regulations between the two jurisdictions;
- A single skills strategy, including higher and further education oversight and planning;
- Acceleration of the second North-South electricity interconnector;
- Improved co-ordination of electricity and other energy markets;
- Co-ordination of policies on environmental protection and climate change;
- Closer connectivity and more joint working between investment promotion bodies;
- Scrapping the need for visas and charges for tourists to Ireland making short visits to Northern Ireland.

CHAPTER TEN
FOREIGN POLICY

Following Brexit, the United Kingdom and the Republic of Ireland have diverged in terms of foreign policy. Those differences include trade, with Great Britain outside the Single Market and Customs Union. The situation is different for Northern Ireland in relation to trade, as it remains within the Single Market for goods and the Customs Union.

At the time of writing, Trump has promised to impose tariffs on EU products, but indicated he may not (though may) impose them on goods from the UK. It is unclear which products will have tariffs imposed and at what size and whether tariffs will be permanent.

The focus may be on EU cars and manufactured goods. Whether that affects pharmaceutical products from Ireland is causing anxiety. Another risk is that the US demands all EU member states remove regulatory restrictions on agricultural imports, which could be severely damaging to the agricultural sector in both Irish jurisdictions.

The United Kingdom government is hoping to avoid tariffs on items sold to the United States, arguing that, unlike the EU, it does not have a trade surplus with the US. However, it too may face pressure to open up its food markets to US food manufactured under its standards. While that might be seen as leading to a lowering of standards, the Trump appointment of Robert Kennedy is expected to lead to a raising of US food production standards. Consequently, this is another area of enormous uncertainty.

Arguments in favour of Brexit had stressed the benefits of sovereignty outside of the EU. However, sovereignty is always mitigated by international agreements, including those relating to free trade. It is possible that the UK now being outside the EU will enable the country to avoid tariffs that the US imposed on the EU. Equally, the

US may strengthen its role as an international bully and demand other trade and foreign policy changes from the UK government to avoid trade tariffs on its exports to the US. The UK may even be treated in the same way as the EU, despite not being a member, especially if the UK attempts to improve relationships with the EU and reduce the trading barriers created by Brexit.

Donald Trump has made clear his strong dislike of the EU, which he has called "an atrocity". The antagonism is connected to the US having a trade deficit with the EU, but is also likely to be EU member states having grouped together to create a counter balance to the US and China – implicitly reducing US global influence. Another factor is Trump's anger at European countries paying a lower percentage of economic output on defence than the US – despite European nations being at stronger risk from conflict with Russia.

Ireland could be specifically in line for trade punishment because of the number of US corporations that have major facilities in the Republic, where they pay much of their tax liabilities. This may (or may not) be mitigated by the supposed affection felt by Trump towards Ireland, where he has a successful golf course at Doonbeg.

Trump has a close relationship with the Israeli government of Benjamin Netanyahu. The criticisms of Israel's war on Gaza and the conduct of that war by both the Irish government and President Higgins may also affect Trump's actions towards Ireland.

The United Kingdom appears to be adopting an approach towards Donald Trump of extreme conciliation. By contrast, Ireland is fully committed to a collective response by the EU, which is likely to lead to retaliation, and threats of retaliation, in an attempt to maintain open trade flows without tariffs. It is unclear which, if either, strategy might be effective over the longer term.

Equally, the introduction of tariffs on global trade may cause significant dislocation of international trade, leading to new consumer price inflation, higher interest rates and a collapse of stock prices leading to a new recession. Similarly, there are suggestions that various stocks – especially crypto assets, but also those of Nvidia and other AI-related companies – are over-valued and could severely fall in market price. A crisis in the crypto markets – which rose sharply after Trump's election – might precipitate a new financial crash or recession.

In short, global capitalism may be about to hit a severe recession. It also might be about to boom. Tariffs may severely damage the Irish and EU economy, but they may also hit the UK economy. Either way, it seems as if the era of globalisation and global free trade is over, with a return to a new form of trade protectionism. How this pans out we will have to wait and see, but much depends on how it does.

David McWilliams has argued that the dire state of UK tax revenues means that it may be shut out of global markets for borrowing, leading to a fiscal crisis that itself could lead towards Irish unity.[156]

Meanwhile – at the time of writing – Reform UK are the most popular British political party according to some opinion polls. Reform UK is a mostly English political party, whose membership is mixed in terms of attitudes to Ireland and probably whether Northern Ireland should stay part of the UK.[157] (Nigel Farage has both said that he expects that it will become part of a united Ireland[158], but also that it will not[159].) Either way, Reform UK is part of a global nativist movement that does not fit comfortably with the politics of much of Northern Ireland and whose English membership may want government more focused on England and reluctant to provide the devolved nations with higher per capita spend than is the case in England.

Seldom have international relationships been so in flux. The ongoing crisis in Ukraine and tensions with Russia have led to pressure to increase spending on the armed services and on armaments. Given Ireland's low defence spending, this could have a serious impact on the Irish fiscal position.

Predictions are extremely difficult and very unreliable at this moment. Yet this is extremely important for the nations involved, but also for the constitutional position of Northern Ireland. If the UK emerges tariff free and undamaged by the US, then many will argue that Northern Ireland should remain within it. But if the EU can protect itself better through its collective strength, then – as with the aftermath of Brexit – more people will lobby for constitutional change, saying that Northern Ireland's future is stronger within the EU via a united Ireland.

CHAPTER ELEVEN
SOCIAL ATTITUDES

At the time of partition, the Catholic Church was in control of the Irish state, just as the Protestant faiths dominated the Northern province. Times have changed in both. Religion is less relevant and less influential – but that is more true in the South than the North. Who, back in 1921, could have foreseen that?

The Catholic Church brought much of its modern irrelevance on itself, through its hypocrisy. There was the Bishop of Galway, Eamonn Casey, who was outed as having had a sexual relationship with Annie Murphy. Subsequent allegations included the rape of a five year old relative, followed by repeated sex attacks on the same girl; other allegations of rape and sexual assault; theft of Church funds; and drink driving. It marked the beginning of the end of Church authority in Ireland.

Subsequent revelations were even worse, none more so than the finding of babies' bodies thrown into old septic tanks by nuns in Tuam. Then there were the stories leaching out of priests conducting sexual abuse of children in Ireland, the United States, Australia, Latin America and around the world. Former pupils of Catholic schools made their own allegations of sexual and physical abuse by priests. The public began to understand the awful reality of Magdelene Laundries and mother and baby homes. So many stories of behaviour by Catholic clergy that breached all their codes left the Church with limited moral authority.

After this, referendums took Ireland into the modern world. Divorce was approved in 1995. Gay marriage in 2015. Abortion in 2018. Ireland had become a different country, one largely irreligious. While many politicians retained their Catholic faith, this no longer controlled or unduly influenced them. And, of course, some of the most senior politicians (including Presidents) had been Protestant, while others were atheist.

By contrast, Northern Ireland is much less socially liberal. Legalisation of abortion was agreed by Westminster, over the head of Stormont – which would not pass laws that met the UK's commitments under an international agreement. Significant numbers of Northern Ireland politicians are socially conservative on matters including abortion, gay marriage, conversion therapy and divorce.

There is a significant divergence between the views of some elected politicians and their own electorate. This is particular true for unionism, with strong differences in social values between younger and older populations making it very difficult for elected politicians to represent the views of their electorates.[160] [161] Whether those tensions in relation to divergence on social values have a significant impact on how people vote in an Irish unity ballot is one of the most interesting questions to be posed in the constitutional debate.

The Good Friday Agreement recognised the deep-seated nature of political and social disagreement in Northern Ireland. It addressed that by including mechanisms to address those disagreements, such as the 'petition of concern'. In many instances, these petitions have been used in relation to differences over social policy: examples include abortion[162] and marriage equality[163]. These applications have been regarded as misuses of a process[164] that was intended to protect the interests of specific communities: ie Protestants/Unionists and Nationalists/Republicans/Catholics.

It could be argued that falling back on petitions of concern where there are differences related, in particular, to social values is defaulting to a position of accepting disagreement, rather than seeking to resolve disagreements by discussion and compromise. However, it is difficult to see how compromises can be achieved on abortion and recognition of gay relationships.

While social attitudes fall outside the simple definitions of religious-based community identities, there is a significant variation with regard to social values between those supporting unionist parties and those supporting others. "Unionist respondents are consistently more on the

Right than respondents who identify as either Nationalist or Neither" according to the results of the Life and Times Survey.[165]

It might be argued that unionist responses are connected to the social attitudes of some of the Protestant organised religions. It might also be suggested that more socially liberal attitudes amongst those coming from a Catholic background are connected to a widespread disillusion with the Catholic Church following a number of clerical scandals. Irrespective of whether both these assertions are correct, they do indicate challenges that will need to be addressed within the debate over Irish unity – and, if there is a positive vote, by the new government in the new Irish state.

The changing demography of Northern Ireland has moved society towards a less religious outlook, more focused on liberal social values. That change is not fully reflected in the political composition of the leadership of Northern Ireland and arguably is more closely aligned to recent governments in the Republic.

CHAPTER TWELVE
THE SHARED ISLAND INITIATIVE

Micheál Martin established the Shared Island Unit in 2020, during his first period as Taoiseach and operating as part of the Department of the Taoiseach. Launching it, Martin said: "In Budget 2021 – through the Shared Island Fund with a planned €500m to be made available out to 2025 – the government is providing the resources to deliver on our commitment to build a shared island underpinned by the Good Friday Agreement.

"The Shared Island Fund will foster new investment and development opportunities on a North/South basis and support the delivery of key cross-border infrastructure initiatives set out in the Programme for Government. It also opens the way for investing in new all-island initiatives in areas such as research, health, education and the environment, in addressing the particular challenges of the North West and Border communities, achieving greater connectivity on the island and enhancing the all-island economy and all aspects of North South cooperation.

"This complements the government's existing all-island commitments, including to the North/South Bodies, to cross-border health services and the Reconciliation Fund, as well as the significant support for peace and progress on the island that will be delivered through the EU PEACE PLUS programme. Taken together, this is a commitment by the government of more than €1bn to investment for the future on an all-island basis to 2025. The Shared Island Fund is central to the government's commitment to harnessing the full potential of the Good Friday Agreement to deliver sustained progress for all communities and traditions on the island."

The three core objectives for shared island investment priorities and all-island partnerships, as set out in the revised National Development Plan, are a more connected island – by investing in enhanced connectivity on the island to enable balanced regional development, sustainable economic growth, recreation and wellbeing; a more sustainable island – by north-south working and investment to protect the common environmental resources of the island, and to address the climate crisis and biodiversity challenges effectively; and a more prosperous island – through co-ordinated investment and co-operation in a number of areas, including research and innovation; higher and further education; and enterprise and tourism, to deliver a more regionally balanced and prosperous island for all.[166] The initiative is also explicitly intended to build a consensus around a shared future on the island.

The main public and political focus of the Shared Island programme has been on the significant capital allocations to important cross-border projects. These include the A5 road (potentially improving the road link between Derry and Dublin), the Narrow Water Bridge, the Ulster Canal renovation and a new teaching and research block for Ulster University's campus in Derry (a commitment under New Decade New Approach of 2020, an agreement which led to the reconvening of Stormont for a period). Funding for a much improved timetable for rail connections between Dublin and Belfast has been very well received.

Infrastructure and environmental programmes are likely to represent a growing element of Shared Island spend, unless there is significant opposition to this from political unionism. "Research and consultation undertaken by the National Economic and Social Council (NESC) for a report and recommendations to Government on Shared Island objectives and opportunities found significant support for an all-island approach to key economic, environmental and wellbeing challenges. In particular, climate change and biodiversity were areas identified as being where all-island action and collaboration would bring greater impact than parallel policies. The Council recommended increased investment in infrastructure to strengthen economic development on all-island and border region basis including in regard to the island-wide energy networks. NESC also recommended expanding the existing collaboration between enterprise agencies to support growth, which informed the development of a new Enterprise Scheme delivered by Enterprise Ireland, InterTradeIreland and Invest Northern Ireland, supported through the Shared Island Fund."[167]

The work of the Shared Island Unit within the Department of the Taoiseach is focused on three activity areas: commissioning research; fostering dialogue; and building a Shared Island agenda, including delivery of commitments in the Programme for Government. It is working with the Economic and Social Research Institute (ESRI), Irish Research Council (IRC), National Economic and Social Council (NESC), Standing Conference on Teacher Education North and South (SCoTENS), and other partners. The first round of Shared Island Fund of research awards was made in 2021. The focus of the 11 successful projects were contributions to new knowledge and perspective to inform the Government's objectives and commitments on a Shared Island, "examining political, social, economic and cultural considerations, underpinning a future in which all traditions are mutually respected".

Deepening beneficial all-island cooperation and enhancing civic connections and understanding are key areas of focus. North/ South and East/West partnership is central to the approach. The programme is providing both a stronger evidence-base along with a rigorous analysis to inform inclusive civic and political discussion on a shared future on the island of Ireland. To date, more than 30 reports have been published as part of the programme: these focus on topics including all-island cancer research; a mapping project comparing law in the two jurisdictions; an all-island approach to tackling hate; fostering constructive and inclusive dialogue between communities; and the effect of Brexit on border communities.

The second round of the Shared Island Fund was made in December 2022, in which €50m was allocated. Of this, €11m was for all-island biodiversity actions, peatlands restoration and biosecurity; €7.6m for new all-island tourism brand collaboration and marketing initiatives; €8m for a Shared Island dimension to the

Creative Ireland programme and cultural heritage projects over 2023-2027; €2m funding contribution to a new Shared Island Civic Society fund, €12m for development of a cross-border innovation hub; and €10m funding contribution to a second round of the North South Research Programme.

The first found of Shared Island civic society awards in 2023 provided funding of up to €50,000 to a range of cross-border collaborative projects, with the largest award going to NICVA. Awards also went for disability sports, cross-border collaboration supporting tourism, environmental protection, to the East Belfast Mission and a project campaigning against violence against women and girls.

In the second round of the Shared Island civic sector awards in 2024, 35 projects were granted funding of a total of €1m. Selected projects have a strong cross-border dimension, facilitating the development of new links and strengthening existing relationships on issues of common concern for civic society groups on both sides of the border.

In truth, while Shared Island is having important positive impacts in discrete areas of activity, the size of funding is too small to have a major effect on the operations of Northern Ireland. It may improve some relationships, but the approach has been to use the money carefully to avoid antagonising political unionism and grassroots loyalism. If the South's government is willing to significantly increase the size of its funding, and ways can be found to reduce anxiety about its use by sections of unionism and loyalism, then it has the potential to improve cross-border trade as well as relationships. At present, though, it is too small in funding to have a major impact. It is an important gesture of goodwill, that might become of increasing significance.

It is reasonable to regard the Shared Island Initiative as being more than a means of improving cross-border relationships. The research funding provides analysis of the differences between the North and South, including pointing up challenges that would need to be addressed if there were Irish unity. While it would be wrong to interpret the funding as a means of creating Irish unity, or even propaganda to promote it, the research programme does provide the basis for planning for unity. This suggests that while the Irish government is not at present advocating for unity or a 'border poll', it is determined not to be caught off guard if one does take place and that leads to a favourable vote.

TABLE 5

Expenditure agreed by Shared Island Fund, listed by size of allocation:

Narrow Water Bridge	€107m
North-South Research Programme	€50m
Casement Park redevelopment (allocation agreed)	€50m
Ulster Canal	€47m
Ulster University, Derry teaching block	€44.5m
Shared Island Enterprise	€30m
Educational attainment co-operation	€24m
Co-centres for research & innovation	€20m
EV charging points	€15m
Hourly rail service, Dublin-Belfast	€12.5m
Cross-border innovation hub	€12m
Peatland & biosecurity	€11m
Battle of the Boyne	€10m
Creative Ireland	€8m
Tourism Brand collaboration	€7.6m
All-island arts	€7.4m
Bio-economy demonstrator	€7m
Local authority development	€5m
Community climate action programme	€3m
Respite centre for children with cancer	€2.5m
Civic Society fund	€2m
Carlingford Lough greenway	€1.5m

Source: Shared Island, Shared Economy, Ireland's Department of Finance[168]

Funding allocations for research projects provide illustrations of areas of concern and opportunity, both today and in the future. Research projects funded under the Shared Island initiative have included:

- An examination of the cross-border institutions established out of the Good Friday Agreement;
- A comparison of higher education in the North West of Ireland with that in Scotland and Wales;
- Early Childhood Education and Care in Ireland North and South;
- Comparing migrant integration in Ireland and Northern Ireland;
- Student Mobility in Ireland and Northern Ireland;
- Changing Social and Political Attitudes in Ireland and Northern Ireland;
- North-South Legal Mapping;
- Cultural Responsivity in Teacher Education;
- Gender and labour market inclusion on the island of Ireland;
- Contrasting housing supply in Ireland, Northern Ireland and the rest of the United Kingdom;
- Calculating the benefit of all-island co-ordination of energy infrastructure and renewable energy supports;
- A North-South comparison of education and training systems;
- An analysis of the primary care systems of Ireland and Northern Ireland;
- Enhancing the attractiveness of the island of Ireland to high value foreign direct investment;
- Cross-border trade in services;
- Social enterprise on the island of Ireland;

- Exploring shared opportunities in the North West;
- Shared Island: Shared Opportunity;
- Shared responsibility across a shared island;
- Reading rooms: fostering constructive and inclusive dialogue between communities;
- Public policy agendas on a shared island;
- Doing feminist legal work;
- An all-island consortium to foster educational neuroscience research and practice;
- Towards an intersectional all-island network for circular bioeconomy entrepreneurship;
- Addressing biodiversity loss with sustainable finance;
- Audience data for cultural policy: a shared island approach to the creative industries;
- All-island rare disease inter-disciplinary research network.[169]

CHAPTER THIRTEEN
THE GOOD FRIDAY AGREEMENT

Strictly speaking, it is the Belfast Agreement, rather than the Good Friday Agreement. However, it is widely, and more commonly, referred to as the Good Friday Agreement, or GFA.

Central to the GFA was mutual respect and equal rights for people from all communities in Northern Ireland. This included the right of people born in Northern Ireland to be regarded as British, Irish, Northern Irish, or all, or any combination, of these. This included the right to hold British or Irish citizenship, or both. There was a commitment to fully respect the civil and political rights, social and cultural traditions, of both communities.

Equally significant was the acceptance by both the British and Irish governments that any decision on whether Northern Ireland should be part of the United Kingdom or a united Ireland must be based on a referendum voted on by the people of Northern Ireland. This was the principle of self-determination for the people of Northern Ireland.

A referendum would be called by the Secretary of State for Northern Ireland once he or she believed there was sufficient support to make it likely that a referendum would lead to a decision supporting Irish unity. Were a vote to be taken and there was support for Irish unity, a confirmatory decision would be taken by Ireland. While it was not made specific it was clear that the referendum result would be by simple majority of those who cast valid votes, while it is assumed that Ireland would also make its decision based on a referendum.

The third core element of the GFA is about how Northern Ireland would henceforth be governed. A new Northern Ireland Assembly would be established, based in Stormont. Those internal governance arrangements were described as 'Strand One'. The second strand of the GFA was focused on internal relationships within the island of Ireland, the North-South institutions. The third strand addressed East-West relationships, not just between Northern Ireland and London, but also between the Irish and British governments.

It was generally assumed that the GFA would lead to a 'peace dividend', with a strong inflow of investment and job creation into the economy. It has instead been observed that this benefit flowed South, not North.[170] While there have been improvements in the Northern economy since the GFA was signed, these have been less than expected. With the benefit of hindsight it is clear that there was less focus in the negotiations than there should have been on economic benefits and on addressing poverty and disadvantage. It has emerged through the release of state papers under the 25 year rule that the Irish government even blocked a proposal to have a North-South body promoting all-island inward investment.[171] The failure to create mechanisms to address economic and skills weaknesses and the embedded poverty in some working class communities continues to be reflected in the widespread dependency on state benefits.

The GFA was agreed by majorities in referendums in both the North and the South. The Irish state changed its constitution as part of this process, removing its territorial claim to the North. (A positive referendum vote in the Republic would need to be followed by a change in the Irish constitution as well – which would require an additional referendum. John FitzGerald has suggested that such a second referendum might not then be carried. Ireland having voted 'yes' in one referendum, but 'no' in a subsequent referendum would clearly create a constitutional crisis.)

Critics of the GFA have argued that its focus was more on ending conflict than on creating a viable and effective system of internal government for Northern Ireland. While this is true, ending the conflict and putting an end to (most of) the related killings was itself a massive achievement after more than three and a half thousand people were killed.

The Stormont system is complex (cumbersome, in the view of critics) in order to ensure fair representation across the two largest communities. Subsequent to its signing the composition of Northern Ireland society has evolved, with more people arriving from other backgrounds and more people born in Northern Ireland not identifying with either the Protestant or Catholic faiths. The GFA did not anticipate this social change, so much of it assumes the continuation of the dominance of these two identities.

The GFA established an elected Assembly, containing MLAs or Members of the Legislative Assembly. MLAs are elected by proportional representation (the single transferable vote). Some of those MLAs were selected to be ministers by the Assembly, using the de Hondt system (with the exception of the justice minister, who must have cross community support). Initially there were six MLAs per Parliamentary constituency, but this was subsequently amended to five MLAs per constituency. MLAs designate as 'unionist', 'nationalist' or 'other'. Where a vote is determined to require cross-community support, both 50% of unionists and nationalists must vote in favour, or 60% of all MLAs vote in favour with at least 40% of the designated unionists and nationalists voting in favour.

Ministers operate through an Executive, led by a designated First Minister and deputy First Minister, who hold equal powers. The GFA, as amended by the St Andrew's Agreement, determined that the First Minister is nominated by the largest party, with the deputy First Minister nominated by the largest party within the other main designation. While the Assembly and Executive can make laws and take decisions relating so devolved responsibilities of finance, health, agriculture, environment, education, infrastructure and justice, various retained responsibilities remain with Westminster, including foreign relations and defence.

The GFA has been amended by the St Andrews Agreement of 2006, while other new agreements have augmented the GFA – the Hillsborough Agreement of 2010, the Stormont House Agreement of 2014, the Fresh Start Agreement of 2015 and New Decade New Approach of 2020.

ST ANDREWS AGREEMENT – OCTOBER 2006

- Introduction of a statutory ministerial code
- Revised pledge of officers requires ministers to fully commit to Executive
- Changed method of appointing First Minister, to be nominated by largest party, and deputy First Minister, to be nominated by the largest party in the other largest designation
- First Minister and deputy First Minister together to place items on Executive agenda, not individual ministers
- Executive decisions to be taken by consensus, or on cross-community basis in absence of consensus
- Created a mechanism, a Referral for Executive Review, for ministerial decisions to be challenged by 30 MLAs
- Created a standing Institutional Review Committee to examine the work of Strand One institutions
- An Efficiency Review to be established to consider value for money outcomes of Strand One institutions
- Prevents MLAs to change community designation unless they change political party representation
- The Executive to support the creation of an Independent Consultative Forum, representing North/South civic society

HILLSBOROUGH AGREEMENT – FEBRUARY 2010

- Devolved policing and justice powers from Westminster to Stormont
- Agreed justice minister to be appointed by a cross-community vote, not via de Hondt
- Affirmed that parties to work together in partnership
- Working groups to be established to resolve problems associated with regulation of parades, how Executive could work better and matters outstanding from St Andrews Agreement

STORMONT HOUSE AGREEMENT – DECEMBER 2014

- Agreement on public sector reform and restructuring
- Agreement on welfare changes
- Establishment of the Commission on Flags, Identity, Culture and Tradition
- Devolution to Stormont of powers to regulate parades
- Agreement to establish a process of reconciliation
- Agreement to establish an Oral History Archive
- Establishment of the Historical Investigations Unit
- Establishment of the Independent Commission on Information Retrieval
- Establishment of an Implementation and Reconciliation Group
- Agreement to reduce number of MLAs per constituency from six to five
- Agreement to reduce number of government departments from 12 to nine
- A protocol to be agreed reforming the Petition of Concern
- Agreement to reform of operation of Executive

FRESH START AGREEMENT – NOVEMBER 2015

- Agreement for Westminster to legislate for welfare reform in Northern Ireland
- Some additional funding for Northern Ireland
- Provides for an official opposition

NEW DECADE NEW APPROACH – JANUARY 2020
- Agreement to settle health pay dispute
- Produce plan to reduce health waiting lists
- Deliver reform of health service
- Increase nursing and midwifery undergraduate places
- Publish a Mental Health Action Plan
- Increase capacity in general practice through multidisciplinary teams
- Improve palliative care
- Fund IVF treatment
- Establish a Graduate Entry Medical School in Derry as part of the expansion of Ulster University's Magee campus to 10,000 students
- Resolve teachers' pay dispute
- Increase resources to schools
- Establish an independent review of education provision
- Support educating together
- Address educational underachievement of children from deprived backgrounds
- Deliver a new special educational needs framework
- Conduct further reform of the Northern Ireland Civil Service
- Review arm's length bodies with aim of rationalising their number
- Develop a regionally balanced economy
- Deliver new infrastructure, including York Street interchange
- Support city and growth deals
- Invest in waste water infrastructure
- Reform licensing laws
- Complete regional and sub-regional stadia programme, including Casement Park
- Tackle climate change, including by reducing carbon emissions
- Develop careers advice
- Develop and implement an anti-poverty strategy
- Tackle paramilitarism

- End sectarianism
- Enable housing associations to build more new houses
- Implement a redress scheme for victims of historical abuse
- Publish a childcare strategy
- Establish a child funeral fund
- Develop a new programme for government
- Strengthen ministers' accountability to Assembly
- Strengthen ministers' accountability for their special advisers
- Publish details of ministers' meetings with external organisations
- Publish details of gifts and hospitality and pay received by special advisers
- Strengthen requirements for record-keeping and the protections for whistleblowers
- Establish a fiscal council
- Reduce use of petitions of concern
- Establish a party leaders' forum
- Create 24 week break after any Stormont collapse before Assembly elections called

[Note: This is not a complete list of commitments]

Subsequent to the GFA being agreed a process of decommissioning of paramilitary organisations began under the leadership of South Africa's Cyril Ramaphosa and Finland's Martti Ahtissari.

The GFA contained within it the principle of review and amendment. Opinion polling suggests that many in Northern Ireland would like its structures to remain, but revised to enable it to operate in a more efficient way. (Retention of Stormont, but reformed, is the most popular option in an opinion poll, attracting the support from most republicans and nationalists, but less than half of unionists.[172]) The failure to recognise 'others', rather than only unionists and nationalists, is the most obvious weakness with regard to contemporary Northern Irish society.

There are also concerns that the joint bodies have failed to operate as effectively or closely as was envisaged.

- The North South Ministerial Council brings together ministers from the Northern Ireland Executive with Irish government ministers. Meetings have achieved less than many had hoped. Meetings have not taken place during times of serious tension and when the Executive and Assembly have not been functioning.
- The North-South Inter-Parliamentary Association is supposed to bring together MLAs with Irish TDs and Senators. It has met on only nine occasions, with gaps between meetings of several years before the most recent event in 2024.
- The British-Irish Intergovernmental Conference promotes bilateral co-operation on matters of mutual interest between the British and Irish Governments, including in relation to Northern Ireland. It has not met since March 2022.
- The British-Irish Council brings together government representatives from Ireland, the UK, the devolved administrations in Scotland, Wales and Northern Ireland and the Crown dependencies, the Isle of Man, Jersey and Guernsey. It has a permanent secretariat based in Scotland, has held 42 summits and last met in December 2024.
- There are six all-island joint implementation bodies: Waterways Ireland, the Food Safety Promotion Board, InterTradeIreland, the Special EU Programmes Body, The Language Body (Foras na Gaeilge and the Ulster Scots Agency) and Foyle, Carlingford and Irish Lights Commission. While these bodies work effectively, they do not cover many of the areas where cross-body partnership is required and might usefully be expanded in number.

In truth, none of the three strands of the GFA has worked as effectively as intended or expected. Nor have they led to the type of engagement across jurisdictions, boundaries and institutions that many hoped. The three strand approach needs to be reviewed and ways found to make it more effective.

Some aspects of the GFA have either never been implemented, or have ceased to be implemented. The Civic Forum has not met since 2002[173], while the promised Bill of Rights has never been agreed, let alone implemented.

Where there has been agreement between the parties, this has not always been positive. The worst instance of arguably improper behaviour and alleged collusion between the two major parties was over the Social Investment Fund[174] – often described as a 'slush fund' to disperse to community groups that the two major parties of the time – the DUP and Sinn Fein – wanted to keep happy. There have been subsequent occasions when ministers have been accused of supporting groups on the basis of identity, rather than approval against clear objective criteria.

Research conducted as part of the Shared Island initiative provides grounds for concern in terms of public attitudes to government in Northern Ireland. While there was a general rise in satisfaction with democracy following 1998 (when the GFA was signed), there has been a decline since 2016. Trust in politics and the media and optimism in the future have also shown declines across Ireland, but especially in Northern Ireland.

There are significant and growing gaps in attitudes between older and younger cohorts, with increasingly positive attitudes amongst older people, but negative ones amongst younger people. Variations also reflect educational outcomes, with more educated groups having more positive social attitudes.

AMENDING THE GOOD FRIDAY AGREEMENT

The Good Friday Agreement was a peace agreement, rather than a blueprint for effective government. It has mostly achieved its objective in keeping the peace, while failing to produce a 'Peace Dividend' of substance or creating a society that is reconciled or economically thriving. The most significant failing of the GFA is that Stormont has been down for 40% of the time since it was agreed. The other issue is that Stormont is so dysfunctional that government operates very badly – most obviously in the case of the health and social care system.

While strong support has been stated for the GFA[175], there is a serious risk of that support waning as it is recognised as a very flawed model of government.

A project from the Constitution Unit reviewing the GFA summarised its findings: "It is a unique and carefully constructed document, and it is the cornerstone of consensual politics on these islands. Its greatest legacy is peace. But the passage of time has revealed weaknesses in implementing areas of the Agreement, which Brexit has exposed further. While the Agreement has had many successes, some aspects have not functioned as imagined in 1998, or indeed been implemented at all."[176]

That full report provides a useful and accurate assessment of where the GFA has left Northern Irish society today: "Violence has been dramatically reduced, and most people in Northern Ireland feel safer, more prosperous, and better able to live easily. Relationships between the communities, as well as political relations across these islands, are also unrecognisably better than they were during the Troubles, or indeed long before that time.

"But that substantial record of delivering peace has not transferred seamlessly to other elements of the Agreement. Strand 1, with the exception of the 2007–17 period, has been prone to frequent collapses. Strands 2 and 3 do function but have not been utilised to the extent envisaged by the Agreement. While there have been successful reforms in areas such as policing and equality legislation, several elements of the Agreement have not materialised or been sustained, including the Civic Forum and Northern Ireland Bill of Rights. Notwithstanding the reduction of violence, dissident republican and loyalist groups continue to exist and exert a wholly unacceptable influence on sections of society."[177]

Most people in Northern Ireland, 55%, believe the GFA should be amended, either some reform (44%), or substantially (11%). About 60% want a Bill of Rights and the Civic Forum. And 58% want the cross-community veto system replaced with a weighted majority rule. Only 37% support the existing mandatory coalition requirement.[178] There is a notable lack of confidence in the GFA amongst younger people in Northern Ireland, with 30% of those under 35 saying they don't know if they support it. Significantly, there is a very low level of trust in the Northern Ireland Executive (17%) and the UK government (21%), compared to the European Union (37%).[179]

The House of Commons Northern Ireland select committee considered the operation of the GFA and made significant recommendations:

"The potential of Strands Two and Three to deliver cooperation on the island of Ireland and across the British Isles has not been realised. While there has been pragmatic cooperation between the Northern Ireland Executive and the Irish Government outside of the North South Ministerial Council and its implementation bodies, there has been insufficient commitment to realising the possibilities Strand Two created, with the instability of the Strand One institutions in turn hindering the ability of Strand Two to function as intended.

"Similarly, the Agreement clearly foresaw the British-Irish Council and the British-Irish Intergovernmental Conference as fora for mutual cooperation on matters of shared interest across the British Isles, but these have often been treated frivolously or as mere support structures for the Strand One institutions. The recently improved relationship between the British and Irish governments provides an ideal opportunity for a broader realisation of Strand Three's scope to address a number of shared policy challenges.

"Recent research, including that which we have commissioned, shows widespread public dissatisfaction with the stability and effectiveness of the Strand One institutions, alongside growing dissatisfaction with cross-community safeguards. While there are mixed levels of knowledge of the possible options for reform, there is clear and compelling evidence that the public are open to change whilst still seeing the Agreement as the only legitimate basis for government in Northern Ireland going forward.

"We contend that extensive and sustained public engagement is vital to determining the future of the institutions and we urge the Government to institute a Citizens' Assembly in Northern Ireland to this effect. While the Agreement made specific provision for review and remediation, there has been no comprehensive assessment of the Agreement's success across each of its three Strands, and less still a serious contemplation on the part of the UK Government of how the Agreement, having brought peace to Northern Ireland, might also provide the long term governmental stability that is necessary for its prosperity.

"As such, we call upon the Government, in partnership with the Government of Ireland and in close consultation with the Northern Ireland parties, to commission a formal, independently led review into the effectiveness of the institutions."[180]

Some 27 years after the GFA was signed, is it time for it to be significantly amended? If it were to be amended there are a number of items that should be considered:

- Prevent the collapse of government and Assembly. Is it right that a single party can bring government and parliament to a halt?
- Should it be possible to prevent the Assembly sitting? (by preventing an election of a Speaker, which requires a cross-community vote)
- Recognise the reality that NI has moved beyond two communities based on religions and now has a third community that has no, or other, religion(s).
- Lack of joint working between ministers and departments. Could an enforceable code be created to force departments and their ministers to work together?
- Reforming the institutions. Could a mechanism be created that forces through reforms that are accepted as necessary, yet never actually happen?
- Creating a second chamber. The Civic Forum was intended as a method of consultation with wider society, yet collapsed not long after it was established. Should it be replaced with a revising and reviewing chamber based in Stormont's largely unused Senate chamber? Would this improve decision making

by spotting the Stormont errors, such as RHI?
- Ending the Petition of Concern. Are we ready to move away from the existing blocking mechanism that has been misused on occasion.
- Reduce the number of parties in the Executive. Would the Executive be more effective with less parties in government and more in opposition?
- Bill of Rights. This was promised in the GFA, yet has never happened.
- Reshape the Northern Ireland Civil Service. NICS is widely criticised: should it be reshaped with a legal obligation on officials to work across departments to achieve agreed objectives?
- Can the public sector be reformed to make it more efficient, bringing its size closer to the proportionate levels elsewhere in the UK and Ireland?
- Strengthen the role of outside experts. How could Stormont better use external expertise to create more effective government? Could a new agreement end the Stormont habit of commissioning reviews and pilot projects, but ignoring the findings?
- Increase the number of cross-border bodies. Are there too few cross-border bodies? Should there be bodies for: skills development, along with further and higher education; to develop integrated all-island healthcare; to tackle cross-border educational under-achievement; to integrate environmental management in border areas; to integrate and manage energy use on a cross-border basis, including regulating illegal smuggling of fossil fuels and monitoring air pollution from fossil fuel burning; to plan public transport provision on a cross-border basis; to integrate infrastructure planning and achieve cost benefits through that planning.

- Strands two and three of the GFA have not worked as well as had been expected, in part because Stormont had been down so much of the time, while in the wake of Brexit relations between the British and Irish government were severely damaged, undermining the capacity for their ministers to come together. Would mandated timetables for strand two and three meetings address this?

Without a review and reform of the GFA, it is difficult to see Stormont becoming an effective system of government for Northern Ireland. That, in turn, will undermine attempts at reconciliation and building social bonds that go beyond the main two rival traditions.

Unionists need to recognise that the status quo builds momentum for those who seek Irish unity – the narrative of Stormont ruling a failed state. As their fallback position, if unionists want Stormont to be retained within a federated united Ireland following a yes vote in a referendum, then they must take some responsibility for getting Stormont to work.

Some republicans and nationalists may lazily believe that all they have to do to create Irish unity is to allow Stormont to continue to fail to deliver effective and efficient government. If they believe that, they are wrong. Voters in the South continue to favour Irish unity, but – according to opinion polls – they are fearful of the costs of harmony and of seeking to absorb a society that is not at ease with itself and in which parts of unionism is refusing to help to make work.

The reality of Northern Ireland is that it is a divided society in which the members of the two main traditions plus the others need to find ways to work together that deliver for the whole of that society. Twenty seven years after the GFA, that outcome has yet to be achieved.

CHAPTER FOURTEEN
WHAT MIGHT IRISH UNITY ACHIEVE?

Driving across a border road is instructive. In years gone by, as you crossed from the North to the South you would notice an immediate deterioration, a symbol of travelling into a poorer nation. Today that symbolism is reversed – the pot holes proliferate in the North, are less common in the South, while the road surfaces seem generally superior in the Republic.

The quality of road surfaces is no basis for deciding the constitutional outcome of the island of course. Yet the symbolism is instructive. The South's skills and education system is better suited to a modern economy, which has its rewards (along with those of its tax system and membership of the European Union) in a vibrant tech sector and global investment that the North can barely dream of.

The South has many problems – housing, health, energy and water infrastructure, inequality, environmental damage. But the North shares those problems, some to a lesser extent, others to a greater extent. Some – health and water infrastructure – might be better and more efficiently addressed through either unification or at least greater cross-border co-operation.

Other problems could become worse through unity, however. The most obvious of these is the presence of paramilitaries. While republican paramilitaries are today small organisations, they can continue to disrupt and murder. Loyalist paramilitaries represent much larger organisations, operate as organised criminal gangs and inflict serious damage on loyalist working class communities: the PSNI seems unable to break the organisations or their grip over some deprived communities. It is understandable that some in the South are wary of taking over responsibility for removing these gangs.

The overwhelming benefit of Irish unity would be to move beyond the dysfunctional Stormont system, with its persistent deadlocks and stasis. The structure of the GFA was well meaning, but bakes in an inability to take contentious decisions because of the cross-community veto. That veto has been persistently misused on decisions that are often unrelated to religion or communal identity – regarding Covid pandemic restrictions and a proposal to extend the length of the Brexit transition period[181], for example. The creation of Stormont and the Northern Ireland Executive has put an end to war on the streets, yet perpetuates conflict conducted by other means. Even some senior politicians are unable to put sectarianism behind them.

Yet, if the eradication of Stormont would be the main benefit of Irish unity, why do some seek to create a 'united Ireland' operating on a federal model with the retention of Stormont? Would unity retaining Stormont achieve anything, would it be worth it?

During the Troubles, the Provisional IRA sought to destroy the economic infrastructure of Northern Ireland on the mistaken (and tragic) belief that it would lead to Irish unity. Initially during devolution following the GFA it seemed as if Sinn Fein similarly believed that ensuring the Stormont institutions failed would achieve unity. That strategy, if it existed, also failed.

There is a logic that improving the functioning of government in Northern Ireland will ease the way towards Irish unity as it will reduce the costs of unity and making eventual cohesion more achievable. Sadly, that logic seems to have persuaded some unionists to seek to ensure that Stormont is unsuccessful and dysfunctional. Similarly, efforts to achieve reconciliation and partnership between communities can remain highly contentious and resisted.

How would Northern Ireland change as a place following unity and who would live there? Rejoining the European Union would be a major change and might lead to significant new investment. Similarly, some Irish businesses are likely to take advantage of the opportunity to open new divisions north of the border, taking advantage of lower operating costs. But Northern Ireland is, at present, at nearly full employment, with limited spare capacity in the labour market (in part because of the crisis in the North's health service). This is likely to deter some investment, as would the current lack of capacity in the water and sewage infrastructure. These issues cannot be resolved quickly.

Abolishing Stormont might be one benefit from Irish unity. Others would be the adoption of the Republic's more successful education and skills system, as well as the greater level of investment into the infrastructure that helps to build an effective economy. However, these benefits could take decades to be felt. Another opportunity would be the integration of public services, to reduce costs, improve efficiency and provide better outcomes in both jurisdictions.

And will many unionists follow the proclaimed example of Arlene Foster and leave once a reunification decision is taken? In likelihood, there would be less people leaving than say they would. But the Brexit impact on the British labour market provides some points of reference – large numbers of European Union citizens departed the country, but comparable numbers arrived from countries such as India and the Philippines to fill the gap in employment. If unionists leave, would this be balanced by more workers migrating from the South to the North, to fill vacancies and take advantage of the lower cost of living?

It is not possible to take from the shelf any existing blueprint for successful constitutional change. Various examples can be pointed to in ways that may be helpful. Seamus McGuinness of ESRI has highlighted the length of transition of Hong Kong returning to the control of China – negotiations began in 1982, handover took place in 1997 and integration with the Chinese mainland has been a process that leads to its loss of autonomy in 2047. This was no 'big bang'. Similarly, might agreement be reached with the UK government for a timetable to address matters such as the cost of the subvention?

German reunification happened quickly and with little planning. While some observers have suggested this provides an exemplar for how Irish unity could happen, the omens are not especially positive. While it officially took place in 1989 and 1990, the old East and West Germanys remain socially divided and there was a reluctance amidst parts of both populations to complete unification. Today pay in East

Germany remains around 15% lower than in the West[182] and the neo-fascist AfD party has a strong base amongst disillusioned 'Ossis'.

The initial economic impact of German reunification appeared to be positive, followed by serious fiscal and economic problems. Interpretations differ as to whether this was the result of the burden of the East on the West's economy and fiscal revenues, or whether it was the result of poor fiscal management and the German federal government's determination not to run large fiscal deficits.[183]

We might also consider Brexit, which created a division in what had been a largely single and coherent economic entity. Brexit has exacerbated deep social and political divisions across British society. The refusal by the British government to prepare for the possibility of exiting the EU led to serious difficulties in managing the process. Brexit has led to substantial economic damage.[184] And it took many years longer, with many more difficulties, than the advocates of a 'leave' vote ever conceded would be the case.

The separation of the Czech Republic and Slovakia from the former Czechoslovakia provides limited lessons for other countries. Even as part of one country, the two regions operated in significantly different ways. Following separation they further diverged in their economic practices, before adopting similar strategies as members of the European Union, the euro currency and embedding themselves as part of the Western capitalist system. Improved economic outcomes are therefore more related to those factors than to the constitutional change.[185]

These events suggest that there are different ways to manage constitutional change and those different approaches are likely to lead to significantly different outcomes. In the case of Ireland, it has been assumed that the European Union and the United States are likely to be generous in their support of a new constitutional outcome. At the time of writing, with an increasingly isolationist United States and an EU focused on conflict on its Eastern border, those prior assumptions look optimistic.

Moreover, external events can be as important as the ones that politicians at home can control. Governments are continuing to struggle to deal with the impact of the 2008 recession. The UK is also struggling to deal with the results of Brexit, which might itself be regarded as a response to the pain generated by the recession, as well as the then government's austerity response.

Timing may be just as important as the decision itself.

CHAPTER FIFTEEN
WHAT OPINION POLLING TELLS US

Opinion polling results should certainly be treated with caution – however, in the absence of an actual border poll, they provide the best evidence we have of people's attitudes and intentions with regard to possible Irish unification and also their social attitudes.

In the early part of 2025, the results were released of two important sets of polling. ARINS (Analysing and Researching Ireland, North and South) together with the Irish Times conducted an in-depth polling exercise in late 2024. Less comprehensive, but still interesting, polling was conducted on behalf of the Belfast Telegraph. The results of the two exercises were similar, though not identical.

In broad brush summary, the polls make clear that there are more people in Northern Ireland who wish to remain within the UK than wish to be reunited with the Irish Republic. However, the gap between union and unity is narrowing at a consistent rate and if that trend continues there may be a majority for Irish unity by the end of the decade. The deciding factor may be the attitude of those without a traditional unionist/nationalist/republican identity, given that neither the pro-union nor pro-unity votes now exceed 50% of those polled.

Key results of the two polls were:

- 60% in NI believe it is important or extremely important to plan for a possible united Ireland. (ARINS/Irish Times)

- 34% in NI would vote for Irish unity, up from 30% in 2023 and 27% in 2022. (ARINS/Irish Times)

- 48% in NI would vote to remain in the UK, down from 51% in 2023 and 50% in 2022. (ARINS/Irish Times)

- 64% in RoI would vote for Irish unity, same as in 2023 and down from 66% in 2022. (ARINS/Irish Times)
- 27% of Protestants/unionists would 'hate' losing a border poll on Irish unity. (ARINS/Irish Times)
- 65% in NI and 61% in RoI believe the British-Irish Intergovernmental Conference should continue beyond Irish unity. (ARINS/Irish Times)
- 41% in NI would vote for Irish unity. (Belfast Telegraph/Lucid Talk)
- 48% in NI would vote to remain in the UK. (Belfast Telegraph/Lucid Talk)
- 10% in NI do not know how they would vote and 1% would not vote. (Belfast Telegraph/Lucid Talk)
- 11% in NI want a border poll within three years; 34% in three to ten years; 10% in 11 to 20 years; and 9% within the following ten years. (Belfast Telegraph/Lucid Talk)

(Bill White of Lucid Talk explained that the variation in the number supporting Irish unity – 34% in the Irish Times and 41% in the Belfast Telegraph – can be explained by the polling methodology. The Irish Times uses face-to-face surveys, while Lucid Talk's Belfast Telegraph surveys ae online, which produce fewer 'don't knows'.[186])

In addition, the Life and Times Survey[187] provides relevant demographic information on Northern Ireland:

- 26% of NI people regard themselves as Irish, not British;
- 11% of NI people regard themselves as more Irish than British;
- 17% of NI people regard themselves as equally Irish and British;
- 17% of NI people regard themselves as more British than Irish;
- 19% of NI people regard themselves as British not Irish;
- 8% describe themselves in another way and 1% don't know.

If, therefore, the referendum were to be decided solely on the basis of identity, the result would be likely to be very close based on the Life and Times Survey results. Expectations of Irish unity were similarly close: 39% of respondents regard Irish unity as very or quite likely within the next 20 years, while 36% regard it as very or quite unlikely.[188] However, as with other polling, respondents were not yet ready to vote in favour of Irish unity: 35% would vote for unity, whereas 47% would vote for the union if there were an immediate referendum. (The survey was conducted in 2023.)[189] Aspirations are less clear cut – 35% support long term retention of the union, down from 54% in 2016.[190] Support for Irish unity has doubled since Brexit.

These polling exercises underline not only the importance of preparing for an Irish unity referendum, but also that there is a majority in favour of doing so. Some of the projects funded by the Shared Island unit provide an information basis, without triggering unionist hostility by doing it overtly. However, it does also suggest that a more open debate on unity is now required. We have the information, so let us have a more engaged conversation on unity.

The work initiated by Professor Peter Shirlow of the University of Liverpool putting forward the unionist viewpoint is to be welcomed as the beginning of a wider discussion in which unionists are now engaged. Unionists do no favours for their cause by being silent and allowing the pro-unity cause to dominate by default. Even those of us who believe that the cause of Irish unity is the right one – providing it does not retain Stormont within a federal system – welcome an open debate.

CONCLUSION
PREPARING FOR A BORDER POLL

It is surely more a question of when, not if, a border poll will take place. There is probably universal acceptance that it is essential to avoid a Brexit referendum process and outcome: lots of misleading facts during the debate, resulting in an outcome that almost no one expected and few wanted. During the debate, those involved had suggested the UK might remain within the Single Market and Customs Union; some argued that UK citizens' rights within the EU would be unaffected (they weren't); and there were significant disagreements as to whether the outcome would damage or benefit the UK economy.

With the benefit of hindsight, the Brexit process might have benefited from independent adjudication on the claims being made. Instead, voters tended to believe what they wanted to believe, irrespective of the plausibility of some of the claims. A body – equivalent to FactCheckNI – that verified the competing claims might have an important role both within a referendum debate, but also in the years leading up to a poll.

Expecting or hoping for a future border poll is no justification for not reforming Northern Ireland and its government today. If Northern Ireland truly is the 'basket case' that its republican critics say, then why would voters within the Republic choose to take it on? Could a 'failed and failing state' be turned around simply by changing sovereignty? Especially if the instrument of that failure – Stormont – was to be retained within a united Ireland, as many suggest.

Reform of the Good Friday Agreement is therefore needed, irrespective of whether much of Northern Ireland is seeking Irish unity in either the short or medium term.

Strands one, two and three of the GFA require commitment and engagement by all participants. Intelligent and pragmatic unionism recognises that good relationships between the North and South are mutually beneficial. This is particularly true in border areas, where divisions between the two governments can cause significant problems on a day-to-day level – for example, with regard to economic development, environmental management, planning policies/development control, air pollution and public transport.

The creation of cross-border bodies has failed to address most of these often pressing daily problems. While it is positive to have a cross-border body dealing with waterways, this emphasises the need to address other problems that do not end at the border.

Sinn Fein has repeatedly called on the Irish government to establish citizens' assemblies to consider Irish unity. This seems a very narrow approach. If citizen engagement is to be encouraged, a single assembly to consider the wide range of challenges that comes with preparing for unity will simply not cut it. One assembly dealing with health and social care policy, for instance, would be swamped. Just dealing with cross-border integration of post-cancer recovery support services would be challenging enough on its own.

Nor should health and education services cross-border partnerships wait until constitutional change. Service improvement and cost savings can be achieved now through a pragmatic approach.

It often seems as though political progress is impossible, prevented by a cross-community veto that seems to apply a principle of 'the lowest possible common denominator'. If progress is to be made, the focus has to be on the future – what is best for our children and our grandchildren, perhaps even for ourselves as we edge into very old age.

The Irish government is in a bind. The more it seems to prepare for Irish unity, the more spooked unionism becomes. But fail to prepare and you might as well be prepared to fail, as the British government discovered with Brexit. Many suspect that the Shared Island unit – including its finance of research conducted by ESRI examining South/North differences – is quietly and slowly making preparations and seeking to lift the North's economic and public sector performance, 'just in case'.

But if that is the reality, progress is the speed of the slowest tortoise in the family. Northern performance on such matters as skills development is horribly slow. But how can an outside government provide a positive influence on this, especially at speed? If anyone knows, both the Irish and British governments would like to hear from them.

An example of this conundrum is the role of Ireland's Senate. How would unionism react if a new form of voting was adopted that enable citizens in the North to vote for some (or all) of their number? Similarly, how would unionism react if voting rights for the President were extended to those living in the North? And, if so, should this be only for those with Irish nationality or also those living in the North who are British citizens?

Another question is whether the GFA right for people born in the North to be Irish or British citizens or both should be similarly extended to those born in the South? Presumably this would be required if and when a united Ireland is established – so why not permit that now?

One of the most urgently required debates is the role of Stormont after a border poll. If one of the main arguments for Irish unity is the incapacity of Stormont to provide effective governance, why on earth would it be retained after unity? Alternatively, if the GFA were reformed now in a way that removed the requirement for mandatory coalition could it lead to an effective Stormont that is willing to make tough decisions that benefit the majority of society – even if it involves standing up to vested interests? (I doubt it.)

Not that events are necessarily in the control of those living in Northern Ireland. Britain – specifically the voters of England – will have their own say in the future. English nationalists have, on occasion, expressed the view that it is wrong that more is spent per capita on public services in the devolved nations than in England, which is the main driver of the UK economy. With the rise of Reform UK, might a more right wing UK government decide to cut funding to the devolved nations? If that happens, how will the Northern Ireland population respond? Come to that, how would it respond if the current British government introduces a new round of austerity in response to a widening fiscal deficit?

It is equally true that while the two governments have sought to keep Stormont on the road – Strand One of the GFA – they have tended to neglect their own obligations under strands two and three of the GFA. North-South and East-West relations are as important as internal Northern Ireland relationships and can also help to reset those internal relationships when those are under tension.

None of Northern Ireland's three communities is cohesive: each contains significant divisions. There is hard line and also pragmatic unionism. There are the 'Castle Catholics' as well as committed republicans. But the differences within the 'other' community are massive. As the labour market moved in 2024 towards 'full employment', so it became increasingly dependent on inward migration to fill job vacancies. That inward migrant community contains people with different religions and heritages, who often have little in common with each other. Would Northern Irish society benefit from new community engagement processes to bring these incomers into our society? Would a resuscitated Civic Forum fill that role?

The GFA has been called the constitution of Northern Ireland. The Republic has its own constitution. How would these two constitutions be merged? Surely a process by which they came together would provide clear evidence that a 'new Ireland' would be a 'new start' and a 'new country'. But if Irish voters recognised that a border poll would not simply lead to the South taking over the North, but actually a process of compromise and genuine merger – perhaps then, Southern voters would reject the idea, concluding they are content with what they have.

A constitutional convention that considered all these issues, without being based on the expectation that it would lead to Irish unity, might be one means of addressing these questions. Such a convention would not be over in a weekend and would be likely to take years to consider the raft of issues involved. If so, it should begin soon.

The Shared Island unit, ESRI and various research projects have already provided more information relating to a possible border poll than was the case with Brexit. But how much public understanding is there of what has been researched? How might this be better communicated? And what changes are needed to reflect the findings in new ways of administering public services and making public policy in both the South and the North?

There is a particular need to improve cross-border partnerships and workings, going beyond the existing cross-border agencies established by the GFA. While this would assist with preparation for Irish unity and improve partnerships in the public sector, this would also support the viability of Northern Ireland as either part of the UK, or as part of a new Irish republic. These objectives need not be conflicting in the short term.

Options that can be considered in order to make progress:

1. A review of the three strands of the GFA to enable them to work more effectively.

2. Amendment of Strand One of the GFA to reflect the changed composition of Northern Ireland, recognition of a third community and the ending of the system of mandatory coalition. Meetings under Strands Two and Three to be subject to schedules agreed to by both governments and all relevant political parties.

3. An expansion of the number of cross-border bodies, covering areas that require two jurisdictions to work together to be effective, including environmental protection of border regions; air pollution control; road and urban planning in border areas; skills development and higher and further education provision; and public transport in border areas.

4. An agreed framework on how progress can be made on bi-jurisdictional co-operation on health and social care; education; and infrastructure, with the aims of reducing costs and improving outcomes in both jurisdictions. The Irish government to open up in stages Irish healthcare to residents in Northern Ireland who wish to avail of it.

5. The creation of an elected all-island Assembly, to meet in the vacant Stormont senate chamber, to advise Stormont and the Oireachtas on how to improve joint work and cross-border arrangements.
6. The formation of a permanent Civic Assembly, to provide an oversight function for the Northern Ireland Assembly and its legislation.
7. The enaction of a Bill of Rights for Northern Ireland and the Republic of Ireland.
8. The formation of an advisory body (a constitutional convention) consisting of legal academics and others, to consider the merger of the Republic's constitution, with the Good Friday Agreement (Northern Ireland's de facto constitution).
9. Confirmation by the British government of its acceptance of the Irish government's legitimate role in relation to strategically important matters regarding Northern Ireland.
10. Agreement between the Irish and British governments to align tax, benefits and pensions regulations to facilitate the expansion of cross-border labour markets.

Northern Ireland needs to be substantially reformed – whether it is part of the UK, or within a new Ireland. The alternative may be the one surmised by economist David McWilliams – Northern Ireland is the wayward child in the divorce, for which neither party seeks custody.

Ireland – South and North – is in a process of transition that became inevitable more than a century ago and yet where the final destination remains uncertain. The territory to be navigated is difficult and contains dangers. Ultimately the destination can only be determined by the people of both the North and the South. Their journey – our journey – will be guided most safely if we understand the dangers, but also the opportunities. Knowledge is not just power, but also our compass.

ACKNOWLEDGEMENTS

This work has been commissioned and made possible by Colm McKenna. Thanks to Michael Gallagher, John FitzGerald, John Doyle, Seamus McGuinness and Peter Shirlow for their comments and suggestions, even when in some instances they profoundly disagree with the tenor of the argument. Thanks also to FactCheckNI and John FitzGerald for permission to reproduce graphs in the text. Any errors are the responsibility of the author.

ABOUT THE AUTHOR

Paul Gosling is an author and journalist, who has written for The Independent, Financial Times and most quality Irish and British newspapers. He has been a councillor for a British local authority and worked inside Stormont as a political advisor.

Paul's books include:

A New Ireland – A New Union: A Ten Year Plan

Lessons from the Troubles and the Unsettled Peace (editor)

The Fall of the Ethical Bank

Abuse of Trust (with Mark D'Arcy)

Changing Money

Government in the Digital Age

Financial Services in the Digital Age

SOURCES

1. https://en.wikipedia.org/wiki/A_Protestant_parliament_for_a_Protestant_people
2. https://www.statista.com/chart/29695/share-of-different-religions-in-northern-ireland/
3. https://www.nisra.gov.uk/system/files/statistics/census-2021-main-statistics-for-northern-ireland-phase-1-statistical-bulletin-religion.pdf
4. https://www.bbc.co.uk/news/election/2022/northern-ireland/results
5. https://www.nisra.gov.uk/statistics/census/2021-census
6. https://www.gov.uk/government/publications/the-belfast-agreement
7. https://www.irishtimes.com/politics/2023/10/23/united-ireland-referendum-should-need-super-majority-in-north-republic-to-carry-says-baker/
8. https://www.oireachtas.ie/en/debates/debate/joint_committee_on_the_implementation_of_the_good_friday_agreement/2022-06-30/2/
9. https://www.civilserviceworld.com/in-depth/article/brexit-negotiations-former-number-10-advisor-jonathan-powell-on-how-to-get-the-deal-done
10. BBC interview, link at https://www.presstv.ir/Detail/2020/01/25/617088/UK-Scotland-Glasgow-Irish-Unity-Parade
11. https://www.gov.uk/government/publications/the-st-andrews-agreement-october-2006
12. https://www.holywelltrust.com/forward-together-podcast/gfa-analysis-opens-new-podcast-series
13. https://www.irishtimes.com/ireland/2024/12/30/irish-officials-requested-that-inward-investment-be-kept-out-of-north-south-co-operation/
14. https://www.theyworkforyou.com/ni/?id=2013-03-19.5.1&s=speaker%3A13836
15. https://aims.niassembly.gov.uk/questions/writtensearchresults.aspx?&qf=0&qfv=1&ref=AQW%208613/17-22
16. https://x.com/GlenMillerUUP/status/1831257345000644853
17. https://fullfact.org/europe/our-eu-membership-fee-55-million/
18. https://d3nkl3psvxxpe9.cloudfront.net/documents/YouGov_-_Conservative_members_poll_190614.pdf
19. https://fedtrust.co.uk/nationalisms-in-the-uk-and-the-implications-for-the-westminster-system-of-governance/
20. https://www.ons.gov.uk/peoplepopulationandcommunity/culturalidentity/ethnicity/bulletins/nationalidentityenglandandwales/census2021#:~:text=15.3%25%20of%20people%20selected%20an,or%20 42.2%20million%2C%20in%202011)
21. https://www.belfasttelegraph.co.uk/news/politics/one-day-there-will-be-a-united-ireland-claims-brexiteer-and-former-mep-nigel-farage/a217279530.html

22 https://www.newsletter.co.uk/news/politics/i-do-not-think-an-all-ireland-is-likely-and-i-am-not-sinn-feins-friend-says-nigel-farage-in-riposte-to-lord-empey-4357001

23 https://www.bbc.co.uk/news/articles/c20m1ejj00vo

24 https://www.bbc.co.uk/news/articles/cw89lje5q7do

25 https://www.ulster.ac.uk

26 https://datavis.nisra.gov.uk/economy-and-labour-market/labour-market-report-february-2025.html#

27 https://www.investni.com/media-centre/news/murphy-leads-all-island-trade-mission-singapore

28 Holywell Trust report, North West regional economy

29 https://www.irishtimes.com/business/economy/2025/02/17/northern-businesses-setting-up-firms-in-the-republic-to-benefit-from-lower-corporation-taxes/

30 https://www.ons.gov.uk/peoplepopulationandcommunity/populationandmigration/populationestimates/bulletins/annualmidyearpopulationestimates/mid2023

31 https://www.ons.gov.uk/employmentandlabourmarket/peopleinwork/publicsectorpersonnel/datasets/publicsectoremploymentreferencetable

32 https://data.oireachtas.ie/ie/oireachtas/parliamentaryBudgetOffice/2024/2024-01-23_public-sector-staffing-and-pay-2024_en.pdf

33 https://www.cso.ie/en/releasesandpublications/ep/p-cpsr/censusofpopulation2022-summaryresults/populationchanges/#:~:text=On%20Census%20Night%2C%20Sunday%2C%2003,population%20of%20Ireland%20was%205%2C149%2C139.

34 https://www.communities-ni.gov.uk/publications/northern-ireland-housing-statistics-2023-24

35 Emailed statement to author from NI Water

36 https://www.irishtimes.com/ireland/education/2024/11/13/ireland-has-highest-rate-of-third-level-education-in-eu/

37 https://www.nisra.gov.uk/system/files/statistics/Qualifications-in-northern-ireland-2020.pdf

38 https://www.nuffieldfoundation.org/news/new-study-compares-pupil-performance-across-uk-nations

39 https://www.esri.ie/news/esri-research-examines-educational-systems-and-outcomes-in-ireland-and-northern-ireland-from

40 https://www.belfastcity.gov.uk/getmedia/1d2a917d-3d3f-4f74-a29e-c8d360a0c83d/POP008_TP-Pop.pdf

41 https://www.nisra.gov.uk/news/good-jobs-northern-ireland-2024

42	https://www.thegeographist.com/uk-cities-population-100/
43	http://www.citymayors.com/gratis/uk_topcities.html
44	https://www.bbc.co.uk/news/uk-northern-ireland-67717507
45	https://www.daera-ni.gov.uk/articles/mobuoy-remediation-project
46	https://www.bbc.co.uk/news/uk-northern-ireland-66789885
47	https://www.bbc.co.uk/news/uk-northern-ireland-68398439
48	https://www.bbc.co.uk/news/articles/c4gdp0wry9no
49	https://www.nipolicingboard.org.uk/questions/what-are-psni-officer-numbers-year-year-2001
50	https://www.bbc.co.uk/news/articles/c4gdp0wry9no
51	https://cain.ulster.ac.uk/issues/police/patten/patten99.pdf
52	https://www.amnesty.org.uk/press-releases/landmark-case-press-freedom-northern-ireland-and-met-police-broke-law-spying
53	https://www.niauditoffice.gov.uk/files/niauditoffice/media-files
54	https://www.bbc.co.uk/news/uk-northern-ireland-23706899
55	https://www.oecd.org/en/publications/government-at-a-glance-2023_3d5c5d31-en.html
56	https://thedocs.worldbank.org/en/doc/0274411350395ce53ccd3e91a431e924-0050022024/original/FINAL-ICP-2021-Global-and-regional-highlights.pdf
57	https://www.imd.org/centers/wcc/world-competitiveness-center/rankings/world-competitiveness-ranking/rankings/wcr-rankings/
58	https://thedocs.worldbank.org/en/doc/0274411350395ce53ccd3e91a431e924-0050022024/original/FINAL-ICP-2021-Global-and-regional-highlights.pdf
59	https://www.economicsobservatory.com/how-did-ireland-recover-so-strongly-from-the-global-financial-crisis
60	https://www.cso.ie/en/releasesandpublications/ep/p-vsys/vitalstatisticsyearlysummary2014/
61	https://www.cso.ie/en/releasesandpublications/ep/p-pme/populationandmigrationestimatesapril2024/keyfindings/
62	https://www.nisra.gov.uk/publications/census-2021-main-statistics-demography-tables-age-and-sex
63	https://www.nisra.gov.uk/publications/2011-census-key-statistics-tables-demography
64	https://www.nisra.gov.uk/publications/2011-census-key-statistics-tables-demography
65	https://publications.parliament.uk/pa/ld200708/ldselect/ldeconaf/82/82.pdf

66. https://committees.parliament.uk/writtenevidence/87632/pdf/
67. https://cepr.org/voxeu/columns/economic-impacts-immigration-uk
68. https://www.bma.org.uk/advice-and-support/gp-practices/managing-workload/safe-working-for-gps-in-northern-ireland
69. https://www.bbc.co.uk/news/uk-northern-ireland-65843975
70. BMA, ibid
71. https://datavis.nisra.gov.uk/economy-and-labour-market/labour-market-report-january-2024.html
72. https://www.ons.gov.uk/employmentandlabourmarket/peopleinwork/employmentandemployeetypes/bulletins/uklabourmarket/latest
73. https://www.ons.gov.uk/employmentandlabourmarket/peoplenotinwork/economicinactivity/datasets/economicinactivitybyreasonseasonallyadjustedinac01sa
74. https://www.bbc.co.uk/news/uk-northern-ireland-64971161
75. https://www.phin.org.uk/news/private-market-update-december-2022
76. https://www.health-ni.gov.uk/sites/default/files/publications/health/expert-panel-full-report.pdf
77. https://data.oireachtas.ie/ie/oireachtas/committee/dail/32/committee_on_the_future_of_healthcare/reports/2017/2017-05-30_slaintecare-report_en.pdf
78. https://www2.hse.ie/services/schemes-allowances/medical-cards/about-the-medical-card/prescription-charges/#:~:text=If%20you%20are%20under%20the,for%20each%20person%20or%20family.
79. https://www.citizensinformation.ie/en/health/health-services
80. https://www.gov.ie/en/publication/6a6b5-national-healthcare-statistics-2023/
81. ESRI
82. https://factcheckni.org/articles/are-nis-hospital-waiting-lists-over-twice-as-long-as-they-are-in-ireland/
83. https://www.esri.ie/news/new-esri-research-compares-productivity-levels-in-ireland-and-northern-ireland
84. https://www.esri.ie/news/brexit-reduced-overall-eu-uk-goods-trade-flows-by-almost-one-fifth
85. https://www.esri.ie/news/new-esri-research-highlights-strong-trade-relationship-between-ireland-and-northern-ireland
86. https://www.esri.ie/news/shift-in-irish-imports-from-great-britain-to-northern-ireland-due-to-brexit
87. https://www.belfastcity.gov.uk/investinbelfast/connections/news/northern-ireland-targets-roi-investors-with-lure-o
88. https://www.belfasttelegraph.co.uk/business/technology/derry-still-a-big-draw-for-the-tech-sector/41249344.html

89 https://www.esri.ie/news/new-esri-and-niesr-macroeconomic-model-for-northern-ireland-can-be-used-to-analyse-potential
90 https://www.esri.ie/system/files/publications/RS198.pdf
91 https://www.esri.ie/news/new-esri-research-examines-what-factors-influence-housing-supply-in-ireland-northern-ireland
92 https://www.esri.ie/news/new-research-shows-aligned-renewable-energy-targets-for-ireland-and-northern-ireland-supports
93 https://www.esri.ie/news/children-in-large-families-in-lone-parent-households-and-in-households-where-someone-has-a
94 https://www.esri.ie/news/shared-island-esri-report-examines-why-income-inequality-is-similar-in-ireland-and-northern
95 https://www.esri.ie/news/shared-island-esri-report-sheds-light-on-gender-disparities-in-the-labour-market-across-the
96 https://www.communities-ni.gov.uk/sites/default/files/2024-11/dfc-consultation-gender-pay-gap-info-regs.pdf
97 https://www.esri.ie/news/new-esri-research-highlights-high-employment-among-migrants-in-ireland-and-northern-ireland
98 https://www.esri.ie/news/families-in-northern-ireland-more-reliant-on-family-and-friends-for-childcare-than-those-in
99 https://www.esri.ie/news/esri-research-on-education-systems-north-and-south-to-be-discussed-at-belfast-event
100 https://www.esri.ie/news/esri-research-examines-educational-systems-and-outcomes-in-ireland-and-northern-ireland-from
101 https://www.esri.ie/news/esri-publishes-report-examining-primary-healthcare-on-the-island
102 Shared Island, Shared Economy: Comparison of economic structures and linkages between Ireland and Northern Ireland June 2024
103 might have been prevented if timely and effective primary care was provided), neither system
104 https://www.ulster.ac.uk/__data/assets/pdf_file/0009/1678122/Summer-Outlook-2024-Update.pdf
105 https://muse.jhu.edu/article/853103
106 https://muse.jhu.edu/pub/423/article/908962
107 https://pure.ulster.ac.uk/ws/portalfiles/portal/91680837/isia.2021.32b.43.pdf
108 https://sluggerotoole.com/2018/11/24/healthcare-in-a-new-ireland/
109 https://pure.ulster.ac.uk/ws/portalfiles/portal/91680837/isia.2021.32b.43.pdf
110 https://www.psni.police.uk/sites/default/files/2024-12/Cross%20Border%20Policing%20Strategy%202025-2027.pdf
111 https://committees.parliament.uk/publications/5650/documents/55754/default/

112 https://www.esri.ie/news/esri-research-examines-educational-systems-and-outcomes-in-ireland-and-northern-ireland-from

113 https://www.bbc.co.uk/news/articles/ckgr84vdep5o

114 https://publicpolicy.ie/environment/linking-the-irish-environment-exploring-the-role-of-civil-society-in-promoting-cross-border-environmental-cooperation/

115 https://www.iiea.com/images/uploads/resources/Northern_Ireland_Subvention_Possible_Unification_Effects.pdf

116 https://www.thebritishacademy.ac.uk/documents/3854/98p035.pdf

117 https://www.thebritishacademy.ac.uk/documents/3854/98p035.pdf

118 https://pureadmin.qub.ac.uk/ws/portalfiles/portal/507126650/When_worse_is_better.pdf

119 https://cain.ulster.ac.uk/ni/economy.htm

120 https://www.ons.gov.uk/economy/governmentpublicsectorandtaxes/publicsectorfinance/datasets/countryandregionalpublicsectorfinancesnetfiscalbalancetables

121 ESRI

122 https://www.economicsobservatory.com/the-good-friday-agreement-at-25-has-there-been-a-peace-dividend

123 https://www.economicsobservatory.com/the-good-friday-agreement-at-25-has-there-been-a-peace-dividend

124 Why the 'subvention' does not matter: Northern Ireland and the all-Ireland economy. Irish Studies in International Affairs, 32 (2). pp. 314-334. ISSN 2009-0072

125 https://doras.dcu.ie/28451/1/project_muse_810176.pdf

126 https://www.gov.ie/en/publication/09fbf-shared-island-shared-economy-comparison-of-economic-structures-and-linkages-between-ireland-and-northern-ireland/

127 https://www.gov.ie/en/publication/09fbf-shared-island-shared-economy-comparison-of-economic-structures-and-linkages-between-ireland-and-northern-ireland/

128 https://muse.jhu.edu/article/810176/pdf

129 https://muse.jhu.edu/pub/423/article/913623/pdf

130 https://docs.iza.org/dp12496.pdf

131 https://www.irishnews.com/news/northern-ireland/united-ireland-could-cost-22-billion-in-welfare-payments

132 https://www.gov.scot/publications/scottish-government-position-on-pensions-in-an-independent-scotland-foi-release/

133 https://assets.publishing.service.gov.uk/media/5a7dc6b0ed915d2acb6ee11f/2902216_ScotlandAnalysis_Conclusion_acc2.pdf

134 https://x.com/DarranMarshall/status/1882741806561190395

135 https://ifs.org.uk/articles/will-be-biggest-tax-raising-parliament-record

136 https://www.cer.eu/sites/default/files/insight_JS_costbrexit_21.12.22.pdf

137 https://www.briefingsforbritain.co.uk/what-impact-is-brexit-having-on-the-uk-economy/

138 https://cepr.org/voxeu/columns/impact-brexit-uk-economy-reviewing-evidence

139 https://niesr.ac.uk/publications/revisiting-effect-brexit?type=global-economic-outlook-topical-feature

140 https://www.prospectmagazine.co.uk/ideas/economics/40005/and-so-the-appalling-human-consequences-of-the-austerity-experiment-become-clear

141 https://natcen.ac.uk/news/half-britain-wants-voting-system-change-clear-majority-among-labour-supporters

142 https://www.esri.ie/system/files/publications/RS198.pdf

143 https://intertradeireland.com/insights/trade-statistics#:~:text=Total%20trade%20in%20goods%20was,Economic%20Trade%20Statistics%20(NIETS).

144 'All island market offers opportunity and challenges on both sides of the border', Irish Times, 28 February, 2025

145 Shared Island, Shared Economy: Comparison of economic structures and linkages, Department of Finance, Government of Ireland

146 BBC interview, link at https://www.presstv.ir/Detail/2020/01/25/617088/UK-Scotland-Glasgow-Irish-Unity-Parade

147 https://hansard.parliament.uk/Commons/2024-12-06/debates/B08DB9F5-4468-4302-B855-A44CCEBE509F/EuropeanUnion(WithdrawalArrangements)Bill#contribution-CFD64B51-67B4-42E2-AA13-E9334DB7322B

148 https://hansard.parliament.uk/Commons/2024-12-06/debates/B08DB9F5-4468-4302-B855-A44CCEBE509F/EuropeanUnion(WithdrawalArrangements)Bill#contribution-CFD64B51-67B4-42E2-AA13-E9334DB7322B

149 https://www.gov.ie/en/publication/09fbf-shared-island-shared-economy-comparison-of-economic-structures-and-linkages-between-ireland-and-northern-ireland/

150 https://www.gov.ie/en/publication/09fbf-shared-island-shared-economy-comparison-of-economic-structures-and-linkages-between-ireland-and-northern-ireland/

151 https://www.gov.ie/en/publication/09fbf-shared-island-shared-economy-comparison-of-economic-structures-and-linkages-between-ireland-and-northern-ireland/

152 https://crossborder.ie/reports/all-island-labour-market/

153 https://www.gov.ie/en/publication/09fbf-shared-island-shared-economy-comparison-of-economic-structures-and-linkages-between-ireland-and-northern-ireland/

154 https://factcheckni.org/topics/europe/do-30000-people-cross-ireland-northern-ireland-border-daily/
155 https://www.cbi.org.uk/media-centre/articles/ibec-cbi-northern-ireland-all-island-economy-conference-to-discuss-new-opportunities-to-maximise-economic-benefits-from-cross-border-cooperation/
156 https://x.com/davidmcw/status/1883092544277615038
157 https://yougov.co.uk/politics/articles/29234-brits-increasingly-dont-care-whether-northern-irel
158 https://www.belfasttelegraph.co.uk/news/politics/one-day-there-will-be-a-united-ireland-claims-brexiteer-and-former-mep-nigel-farage/a217279530.html
159 https://www.newsletter.co.uk/news/politics/i-do-not-think-an-all-ireland-is-likely-and-i-am-not-sinn-feins-friend-says-nigel-farage-in-riposte-to-lord-empey-4357001
160 https://news.liverpool.ac.uk/2015/09/11/new-generation-in-northern-ireland-views-politics-differently-survey-reveals/
161 https://www.theguardian.com/uk-news/2017/aug/04/northern-irish-unionist-parties-alienating-young-protestants-study
162 https://caj.org.uk/wp-content/uploads/2021/06/Briefing-note-on-the-NI-Ministers-Elections-and-PoC-Bill-HC-2nd-Reading.pdf
163 https://www.thedetail.tv/articles/stormont-s-petition-of-concern-used-115-times-in-five-years
164 https://www.niassembly.gov.uk/globalassets/documents/raise/knowledge_exchange/briefing_papers/series3/schwartz200314.pdf
165 https://www.ark.ac.uk/ARK/sites/default/files/2024-06/update154.pdf
166 http://files.nesc.ie/nesc_reports/en/157_shared_island_comprehensive.pdf
167 https://www.gov.ie/en/publication/09fbf-shared-island-shared-economy-comparison-of-economic-structures-and-linkages-between-ireland-and-northern-ireland/
168 https://www.gov.ie/en/publication/09fbf-shared-island-shared-economy-comparison-of-economic-structures-and-linkages-between-ireland-and-northern-ireland/
169 https://www.gov.ie/pdf/?file=https://assets.gov.ie/283234/98e10ee2-7800-48f5-8922-d36990ac3443.pdf#page=null
170 https://www.irishtimes.com/opinion/2023/06/10/david-mcwilliams-the-purpose-of-21st-century-ireland-is-prosperity-the-north-has-red-white-and-blue-poverty/
171 https://www.irishtimes.com/ireland/2024/12/30/irish-officials-requested-that-inward-investment-be-kept-out-of-north-south-co-operation/
172 https://www.ark.ac.uk/ARK/sites/default/files/2024-06/update155.pdf

173 https://www.niassembly.gov.uk/globalassets/documents/raise/publications/2013/assembly_exec_review/10913.pdf

174 https://www.niauditoffice.gov.uk/publications/html-document/social-investment-fund

175 https://cdn.cloud.prio.org/files/d0272813-3889-4ee6-8385-4782a01b896b/Dyrstad%20et%20al%20-%20Public%20Support%20for%20Peace%20Agreements%20Conflict%20Trends%205-2016.pdf?inline=true

176 https://www.ucl.ac.uk/constitution-unit/research-areas/nations-and-regions/perspectives-belfastgood-friday-agreement

177 https://www.ucl.ac.uk/constitution-unit/sites/constitution_unit/files/205_-_perspectives_on_the_belfast_good_friday_agreement.pdf

178 https://www.chathamhouse.org/publications/the-world-today/2023-04/its-time-fix-good-fridaybelfast-agreement

179 https://www.qub.ac.uk/News/Allnews/2023/7outof10thinkthe1998AgreementremainsgoodforNorthernIreland.html

180 https://committees.parliament.uk/publications/42405/documents/210752/default/

181 https://caj.org.uk/wp-content/uploads/2021/06/Briefing-note-on-the-NI-Ministers-Elections-and-PoC-Bill-HC-2nd-Reading.pdf

182 https://www.ifo.de/en/press-release/2023-10-18/differences-economic-structure-explain-wage-gap-eastern-western-germany#:~:text=Today%2C%2033%20years%20after%20reunification,figure%20is%20only%205%20percent.

183 https://www.levyinstitute.org/pubs/hili67a.pdf

184 https://obr.uk/forecasts-in-depth/the-economy-forecast/brexit-analysis/#assumptions

185 https://www.rbinternational.com/en/raiffeisen/blog/market-trends/30-years-of-independence.html#:~:text=Still%2C%20the%20initial%20gap%20was,only%20about%201.15%20times%20higher.

186 'Why do different polls say different things on Irish unity vote?', Bill White, Belfast Telegraph, 24 February, 2025

187 https://www.ark.ac.uk/nilt/2023/Political_Attitudes/IRBRIT.html

188 https://www.ark.ac.uk/nilt/2023/Political_Attitudes/UNTDIREL.html

189 https://www.ark.ac.uk/nilt/2023/Political_Attitudes/REFUNIFY.html

190 https://www.qub.ac.uk/News/Allnews/2023/7outof10thinkthe1998AgreementremainsgoodforNorthernIreland.html